LEGACY OF THE KINGS
LEGENDS OF THE NORTH

Copyright

Ⓒ

Bucur Loredan 13-11-2024
Birmingham U.K.

Prologue:

In the far North,where mountains meet deep fjords and forests seem endless,the kingdoms of Iskali and Fjallgard chose to unite through the marriage of their heirs,Freyja and Eirik. This alliance promised peace and prosperity in a North otherwise torn by rivalries and conflicts.But a betrayal would overshadow these peaceful times:Sigvard,the king's exiled brother, made a pact with King Halvard of Vornheim,a ruler whose ambition knew no bounds and who dreamed of subjugating the entire region.In a series of legendary battles,the five kingdoms of the North - Skoglund,Vintergard,Stormheim,Iskeborg and Solvik,joined forces against Vornheim,ending Halvard's reign and re-strengthening the Nordic alliance.After the victory, peace seemed to have been restored,but King Arvid,heir to a still Northern troubled by the echoes of the past,he knows that such a peace must be consolidated.In search of a queen,he is looking for a princess who is not only beautiful,but also wise and brave,who will help him keep the unity of the five kingdoms and write a new page in the history of the North.

Contents:

Prologue
Chapter 1-Description of the Kingdoms of Iskali and Fjallgard

Chapter -2 The Marriage Proposal Causing Unrest in Vornheim Kingdom
Chapter -3 Wandering Brother Sigvard Joins King Halvard Ruler of Vornheim Kingdom
Chapter -4 Betrayal comes from Vornheim Kingdom

Chapter -5 The union of the two friendly kingdoms through the marriage of Prince Eirik and Princess Freyja

Chapter -6 Revenge of the Prodigal Son Sigvard

Chapter-7 Kingdom of Fjallgard-Iskali

Chapter-8 Legends of the North

Chapter-9 An Ancient Prophecy, The Eye of the Gods

Chapter-10 Liv and Arvid Future Monarchs

Chapter-11 King Eirik and Queen Freyja, completed their journey in this world

Chapter-12 Kingdom of Vintergard and Kingdom of Stormheim

Chapter-13 Kingdom of Iskeborg and Kingdom of Skoglund

Chapter-14 Marriage of King Arvid to Princess Liv of Skoglund
Epilogue

Chapter 1-Description of the Kingdoms of Iskali and Fjallgard

In an isolated corner of the north,covered by vast forests, snowy mountains and deep lakes,lie two magnificent kingdoms:the Kingdom of Iskali,led by the royal family of Princess Freyja,and the Kingdom of Fjallgard,where Prince Eirik and his family rule.These two kingdoms,separated by mountain ranges and a dry river that meanders through plains and forests,have always been united by mutual respect,but keeping a polite distance,specific to these northern lands.The kingdom of Iskali,under the wise leadership of King Alvar and Queen Sigrid,is a land of cold and wild beauty.With fields covered with wild flowers and mysterious forests hiding in them herds of deer and wolves,Iskali is known for its natural beauty,wealth of resources and traditions kept sacred for centuries.The castle from Iskali is an imposing building of white stone,with tall towers rising to the sky,the place from where the royal family watches over the kingdom.Princess Freyja also lives here,a 19-year-old young woman with eyes as blue as ice and long,blond hair,which falls in waves on her shoulders.Freyja is known not only for her beauty,but also for her gentle heart, adventurous spirit and courage.She is loved by the people of the kingdom,always being seen participating in celebrations and activities with the villagers.Freyja he starts each day early,with the sound of the bell ringing through the castle courtyard.After he wakes up and draws his curtains,letting the cold morning light into his room,he begins his routine.A maid brings him breakfast,a plate of fresh bread,goat cheese and a steaming cup of Nordic herbal tea.Dressed in traditional clothes of wool and leather, she puts on her thick cloak and reindeer skin boots,preparing for one of her favorite activities:Riding.Leaving the castle,Freyja meets her horse,a stallion named Sigr,with a coat as white as snow.Together they set off on an adventure,crossing blooming fields,

where yellow and blue flowers dance in the wind. They pass through dense forests with towering firs and pines into the northern sky, while birds chirp overhead, and arrive at the edge of a quiet lake. Here, Freyja pauses for a few moments, watching the reflection of the water, where wild birds rest in groups. King Alvar is a respected ruler, known for his wisdom and patience. A tall man with a white beard and green eyes, the king was always a diplomat, but also a feared warrior in his youth. Next to him, Queen Sigrid, a woman of sober beauty, born of a family of local nobles, is known for her protective spirit and sharp wit. In Iskali, Sigrid is seen as a mother to her people, taking special care of the kingdom's traditions and culture. The two rule Iskali with balance, giving Freyja a example of strength and generosity, which inspires the future leader. Beyond the mountains lies the Kingdom of Fjallgard, a land known for its rapid rivers, waterfalls and snowy peaks. Fjallgard is a harsh kingdom, where cold winds blow incessantly, but the beauty of the landscape is truly remarkable. The castle in Fjallgard is built of blue stone, imposing beauty but also respect, reflecting the character of this kingdom.

In this kingdom lives Prince Eirik,a young man of twenty one years old,particularly strong and brave.With black hair and green eyes Deep down,Eirik is known for his loyalty and ability to fight for those he loves.He is also a skilled hunter and a man of nature,spending hours exploring the forests and mountains of his kingdom.Like Freyja,Eirik has a passion for adventure and spends a lot of time with the people of his kingdom,getting involved in soldier training and participating in local festivals.Every morning,he wakes up at the crack of dawn,and after a simple breakfast of black bread,dried meat, and goat's milk,he takes his bow and starts hiking through the dense forests nearby.This is his way of- and begins the day,feeling connected to nature and the protective spirit of his kingdom.King Ragnar,Eirik's father,is a strong man with a commanding voice and a harsh.Knowledgeable in battle strategies and politics,Ragnar has always been devoted to protecting the kingdom of Fjallgard and maintaining alliances with neighboring king

kingdoms.Queen Astrid,his wife,is an intelligent and calculating woman with a practical spirit and great care for people kingdom.Also an excellent horsewoman in her youth,Astrid shares a close relationship with her son,from whom she has taught him much about nature and strategies for survival.Together,the two rule Fjallgard with firmness and devotion.Thus,in a wild but charming world,the two princes of the Nordic kingdoms grow up under the eyes of their powerful parents, respecting the traditions and values passed down to them.Freyja and Eirik share a love of nature and a heart full of courage,each prepared to protect their kingdom and carry on her family's heritage.Princess Freyja is not alone in Iskali Castle;with her are two close cousins,Tuuli and Aino,the daughters of Queen Sigrid's brother.Although they come from a noble family with origins in the western part of the kingdom,Tuuli and Aino they spent their childhood around their royal cousins and became extremely

close to Freyja,becoming not only her support but soul sisters.The three are almost inseparable,and the presence of her cousins makes the princess feel always surrounded by affection and support.Eighteen-year-old Tuuli is the dreamiest of the three,with golden-blonde hair and green eyes,like the emerald.Although she is charming and delicate,Tuuli has a sensitive nature, loving poetry,traditional songs and art.She is always attentive to Freyja's needs and she sees to it that her cousin has a peaceful and harmonious environment,being the one who tells her old stories and soothes her with verses and songs in the cold nights.Tuuli is known throughout the kingdom for her talent in playing the harp,and the sweet sounds of his instrument often echoes in the castle,calming its inhabitants as well.Twenty-year-old Aino is the older sister and has a brave spirit and energetic,being the one who brings vitality and strength to the group.With brunette hair and sky blue eyes,Aino is a skilled rider and an excellent archer.She has a protective nature,watching over Freyja like a real shield,being aware of her responsibility.Along with Tuuli,

Aino is responsible for their cousin's safety,being the one who,despite her joking attitude,makes sure that Freyja is always well-groomed and protected.Every morning,Tuuli and Aino are the ones who enter Freyja's room with the first rays of the morning.Tuuli opens the curtains and Aino jokes,telling Freyja that "the sun has been waiting for her for a while.

-The two help the princess to her feet,beginning her daily ritual with a small prayer addressed to the Nordic deities,praying for peace and protection of the kingdom.After the maids bring her clothes,Tuuli and Aino help Freyja dress elegantly.They choose between fine woolen dresses and fur cloaks,carefully suited for a day of riding.Tuuli arranges Freyja's hair,leaving it let them fall in natural waves or,on other days,by braiding it into an elegant crown.Aino,instead,catches them at his belt a small engraved dagger,reminding him that "he should never be too far from a weapon.The three then go down to the great hall, where they serve breakfast together.Always,at the table,the girls discuss the day's plans,and Aino often amuses herself by teasing Freyja, saying that she will not be able to keep up with her in the fields.After the meal,they shoulder their cloaks and go out together,with their horses on the castle gate.Tuuli and Aino are always close to the princess when they ride,making sure she doesn't lose sight of her deep in the forest and in the fields.Tuuli talks to her about the plants and flowers they meet on the way,and Aino is vigilant,noticing everything what is going on around them.The three young women often end up at the lake,where they allow themselves a few quiet moments.Tuuli pulls out a water lily flower and arranges its petals in Freyja's hair,laughing and saying that "now she looks more like a goddess Nordic".As the day draws to a close,they return to the castle,where a warm dinner awaits her,served together.Aino often talks about her bow training,while Tuuli reveals her plans for a new poem.

The girls talk about the world around them, about the future and dreams, and Freyja often expresses her gratitude for having them by her side. Tuuli and Aino are not just Freyja's simple companions, but real guardians, protective figures who, despite their young age, understood the importance of their role. They are aware that the safety of the princess and the future of the kingdom depend, to a certain extent, on their care and vigilance, but above all on their unconditional love and loyalty towards Freyja. Alongside Prince Eirik are two cousins of trust: Bjorn and Leif, the sons of Queen Astrid's brother. The two young men are almost inseparable from the prince and represent, in many ways, his support in everyday life, alongside irreplaceable comrades in rigorous training and explorations through the kingdom of Fjallgard. Bjorn and Leif were raised in a family of noble warriors, renowned for their bravery and loyal spirit, values that have been passed down from generation to generation. Twenty-two-year-old Bjorn is the oldest of the three cousins and, at the same time, the most disciplined. With light-colored hair, almost blond, and deep blue eyes, Bjorn is known for his calculating manner and for his penchant for battle strategies.

He is the one who ensures the balance of the group,recalling- and often to Eirik the importance of princely responsibilities.As a skilled warrior,Bjorn is known for his skills with sword and bow,being an excellent instructor and a trusted mentor to Eirik.Leif,on the other hand,is a year younger than Bjorn,twenty-one years old,and is an energetic and impulsive nature.With brown hair and an ever-present smile on his face,Leif is the most cheerful of the three,always ready to embark on a new adventure or face the challenges of nature.Leif is known for his talent on horseback and his agility in rough terrain,often being responsible for the safety of Eirik's routes.Despite his joking nature,Leif is always careful not to let any threat get close to the prince,being loyal and prepared to defend his family at all costs.Eirik's day starts early,with Bjorn and Leif coming to wake him up in the early hours of the morning.As Leif happily lifts the heavy curtains,letting light fill the room,Bjorn he wakes Eirik with his calm but firm voice,reminding him of the training that awaits him.Prince Eirik gets out of bed and greets his cousins,who help him put on the light armor for training,followed by a thick cloak of wool for protection against the cold winds.After finishing their preparations,the three descend into the great hall of the castle to serve breakfast together,discussing the day's plans and tasks.During the meal,Leif often talks about his latest adventures in the forest,trying to convince Eirik to follow him to a new and unknown place,while the more pragmatic Bjorn remembers to advise them both on their training morning and the strategy exercises.After the meal,the three young men go to the stables,where their horses are waiting for them.Eirik takes his favorite horse,a black stallion called Skald,and next to him,Bjorn and Leif get on their horses,ready for training and adventure.They set off together through the kingdom's forests,where Bjorn suggests different battle scenarios and defense tactics,

using the wild landscape as a training ground.Bjorn teaches them to think strategically and be ever-vigilant,while Leif maintains an easygoing atmosphere,cracking jokes and challenging Eirik to races of speed.During the day,they often end up at the banks of the rapid rivers that run through the kingdom of Fjallgard,where they take breaks and analyze together the possible defense routes and strategic points of the kingdom.Leif he sometimes offers to hunt for the meal,showing his prowess with the bow and proving that he is not only an excellent rider,but also a skilled hunter.Bjorn,in turn,discusses with Eirik his future responsibilities and the strategies needed to preserve the kingdom Fjallgard is prosperous and safe.Despite their different characters,Bjorn and Leif fulfill their roles with great seriousness,knowing that Eirik's life and safety often depend on them.Every day,these two brave cousins offer Eirik not only protection,but also unconditional friendship and valuable advice,thus forming a strong and united team.

Chapter -2 The Marriage Proposal Causing Unrest in Vornheim Kingdom

On a bright summer day,the royal families of Iskali and Fjallgard gathered for a festive meal at the border between their kingdoms.Set in a beautiful clearing,overlooking endless mountains and forests,this meeting was long awaited,and the two families carefully prepared it,wishing to show their respect and friendship.A huge table,carved from oak wood and adorned with silk cloths,had been placed in the open air.Along the table were rich platters with game,venison and wild boar meat cooked with rare spices,wild birds stuffed with herbs and berry sauces.On the selected trays there were also seasonal fruits,red grapes and juicy pears,along with fresh black bread,butter and fine cheeses.Chosen wines,brought from the royal cellars,completed the feast,and a royal orchestra played elegant waltzes and medieval dances,accompanying the atmosphere with the sweet sounds of the harp,violins and flutes.Among the guests,Freyja,Tuuli,and Aino were dressed in precious dresses,

each dress being a work of art.Freyja wore a light blue dress,adorned with silver embroidery and a fine cloak that rose slightly in the wind.Tuuli and Aino had golden dresses,decorated with silk thread and fine fur,matching carefully crafted earrings and bracelets.On the other hand,Eirik,Bjorn and Leif wore elegant suits,with long tunics and fine embroidery,each with rich cloaks on their shoulders,symbols of their princely positions.After clinking the first glasses of wine and having served from the chosen dishes,King Alvar and Queen Sigrid exchanged friendly glances with King Ragnar and Queen Astrid.The conversations began with small talk about the kingdoms, their condition,and the good times of peace and prosperity that both nations enjoyed.Finally,King Ragnar spoke,raising a glass of wine and looking directly at Alvar and Sigrid saying:

-Dear friends and allies,for many years we have maintained the friendship between Iskali and Fjallgard,and we have seen our kingdoms grow together in peace and prosperity.But as time passes,we feel that our bond should grow even stronger,to be ennobled and by blood.

For this reason,Astrid and I come today with a proposal that would bring the two kingdoms closer than ever.King Alvar and Queen Sigrid turned their attention,curious,but also deeply understanding the intentions of their friends Queen Astrid continued,looking fondly at Freyja:

-Our son,Eirik,is a strong and brave young man,and Freyja,our dear princess,is a special young woman,valued in all of Iskali.We believe that a union between them would not only bring even more stability and prosperity to the peoples ours,but it would also be a soul alliance between the two.Through their connection,we want our entire heritage and values to be carried forward.Freyja,surprised by the proposal,turned her gaze to Eirik,who,blushing slightly,met her gaze with a shy but sincere smile.Tuuli and Aino exchanged delighted and discreet glances,encouraging Freyja with complicit smiles.On the other side,Bjorn and Leif patted Eirik on the shoulder,saying whispering that this marriage would be an honor both for him and for the kingdom.King Alvar spoke,standing up:

-It is a great proposal,Ragnar,and we know how much such an alliance would mean.Eirik and Freyja are the children of our hearts,and we wish for them a happy and strong future.You,the people of Fjallgard,have proven many times the honor and your courage,and we are honored to unite through the bond between these two souls.Queen Sigrid took Freyja's hand,offering her a gentle smile:
- Our decision is a noble and wise one,but of course,we must also know the wishes of our children.Eirik took the initiative and stood up with a firm smile,looking affectionately at Freyja:
-For me,this union is an honor,and with Freyja I would be more than happy to serve our people,to preserve our peace and values.It would be an honor to have such a princess by my side.Excited,Freyja smiled,bowing gently bowing his head and modestly accepting the proposal.At that moment,the applause of the guests and the sound of royal music filled the atmosphere,beginning a series of dances celebrating the alliance of the two kingdoms.The royal orchestra stepped up its rhythms,singing a series of waltzes and medieval dances,

where Freyja and Eirik were the first guests on the dance floor. Along with them, Tuuli, Aino, Bjorn and Leif joined them, and the whole company spent the evening in an unparalleled merriment. The evening ended with promises of peace and hope, and the alliance between the kingdoms of Iskali and Fjallgard was now sealed by the understanding between two strong families and two young hearts, ready to lead to a bright future. Prince Eirik's older brother was called Sigvard, a young man of 24, whose angelic features and natural charisma made him often admired but also feared in the kingdom of Fjallgard. Despite his ravishing beauty, golden blonde hair, deep blue eyes and perfectly contoured aristocratic figure, Sigvard had a dark side that ended up ruining his position and reputation in the family. Instead of using his skills and gifts to serve the kingdom, he chose to indulge his own desires and pleasures, becoming a notorious womanizer and drunkard known throughout the kingdom. Because of his behavior his uncontrolled and numerous scandals caused, King Ragnar was forced to make a difficult decision:

-Sigvard was banished from the royal court,considered a disgrace to the honor of the family and a threat to the stability of the kingdom.Exiled,Sigvard left the castle and took refuge deep in a dense forest on the edge of the kingdom of Fjallgard,a place shrouded in mystery and isolated from eyes of the world.This forest,known as the "Forest of Shadows",was far from the main roads,and rumors about it described it as a haunted place,where many people disappeared without a trace.After several months of living in the wilderness and isolation,Sigvard and -he found an ally in King Halvard,a feared ruler and his father's greatest enemy.Halvard,the ruler of the kingdom of Vornheim,was known for his boundless ambitions and his desire to conquer the surrounding territories.The kingdom of Vornheim,under the leadership of King Halvard,was one of the most feared and respected kingdoms in the north.Located in a wild and inhospitable region,surrounded by steep cliffs and dense forests,Vornheim was a place of contrasts:as beautiful as nature was,as harsh were the conditions of life.Halvard,the king of this realm,was a remarkable yet feared leader,known throughout the North for his unbridled ambition and fierce desire to expand his kingdom.Halvard was a man of imposing presence.Tall and stout,with with the color of iron and piercing cold blue eyes,the king inspired fear and respect at the same time.He was known to be relentless in battle and merciless to those who stood in his way.To him,his kingdom was above all else something else,and territorial expansion was a mission he considered sacrosanct.Halvard's ambitions knew no bounds;he was determined to leave an indelible mark on history and transform Vornheim into an empire.Halvard had not always been a ruler whose his name caused fear.In his youth, he had been a talented and brave,but also just,warrior.But once he ascended the throne,his desire for power changed his personality,transforming him into a leader obsessed with the idea of supremacy.Halvard justifies his desire of conquest by believing that Vornheim deserved to be the center of all the Nordic kingdoms.He believed that only through a unified kingdom under his rule could the North achieve its true glory.One of Halvard's essential qualities was his ability to plan strategically.The King of Vornheim never went into battle without meticulous preparation and deep analysis of the enemy.Halvard spent whole nights studying maps and listening to the reports of his spies,looking for the weak points of his enemies.He had an extensive network of informers and spies who they provided information on all the movements of the neighboring kingdoms,something that always gave him an advantage in battle.Halvard's warriors were trained by harsh and ruthless methods, thus gaining exceptional resistance.Under his guidance,Vornheim's army had become one of the most well-trained and feared from the North.Halvard chose his generals very carefully,preferring those with battle experience and absolute loyalty to him.

Each war fought was a further step towards his dream of expansion,and Halvard used both brute force and and diplomacy in order to achieve his goals.Halvard was not only motivated by the desire to expand his territories.For him,conquering other kingdoms was also a way to demonstrate his superiority,both to his enemies and towards his own men.The King of Vornheim could not stand the idea of being perceived as an equal by other kings;he believed that his power should be unquestionable.This desire for dominance made him ruthless in battle, without hesitation when it came to-destroy his opponents.Halvard was constantly planning expeditions and campaigns of conquest,and each success strengthened his desire to go further.Over the years,he conquered villages,brought tribes to their knees, and imposed Vornheim control over the surrounding territories.But Halvard's relentless ambition had a side effect:many of his advisors and nobles were beginning to fear the growing power of of the king.But no one dared oppose;Halvard was a leader who did not tolerate weakness or disloyalty.The kingdom of Vornheim was

as harsh as its king.Its landscapes were dominated by rocky mountains,dense forests,and dark swamps,creating a cold and unwelcoming atmosphere.However,this harsh land also had its beauty.Vornheim was known for its rich resources,especially iron and copper deposits, which it mined and used to strengthen its army.The steel forged in Vornheim was considered second to none in the North,and its craftsmen were renowned for their skill.Halvard invested heavily in developing these resources, knowing that they gave him a significant military advantage.Furthermore,the king developed his kingdom not only as a fortress of the army, but also as a thriving economic center.Merchants brought goods from all corners of the North,and Vornheim's craftsmen produced weapons and armor for which demand was always high.Halvard's court was a combination of luxury and discipline.The king was not a great lover of opulence,but he valued wealth and was careful to maintain a level of luxury that would impress visitors and reflect his power.His palace was built of massive stone and

decorated with coats of arms and trophies from battles won, giving it an imposing and cool atmosphere. Although it was not known for his hospitality, Halvard held lavish banquets for his allies, using these gatherings to secure their support and loyalty. In his relationship with his courtiers, Halvard was authoritative and aloof. He could not afford to be vulnerable in front of anyone, and loyalty was an essential condition to be able to remain at his court. Those who betrayed his trust were severely punished, and Halvard made sure that such examples were known throughout the kingdom, as a warning to those who would dare to undermine authority. Although a strong leader, Halvard was not a father who cared about his family in the traditional way. To him, his children were merely potential heirs to his ambitions and successors to his dream of supremacy. He did not involve himself in their personal education, but he ensured that they received the best training in the arts of war and politics so that they would become leaders as powerful as he was. He was known to have a cold and distant relationship with his heirs, whom he instilled in the idea that weakness was not acceptable and that their

duty to the kingdom was more important than anything else.For Halvard,the North was a territory to be conquered and unified under one ruler.He believed that force was the only method by which this unity could be achieved and he distrusted alliances that were not cemented by victory and subjugation.Vornheim,in his view,was the kingdom that deserved to rule over all others,and he,Halvard,saw himself as the man meant to make this dream a reality.His dream of unifying the North under one rule brought him both support and enemies.Many feared his ambitions and saw him as a threat,but no one could challenge his strength and influence.

Chapter -3 Wandering Brother Sigvard Joins King Halvard Ruler of Vornheim Kingdom

King Halvard,a cunning and calculating man,saw in Sigvard an opportunity to destabilize the royal family of Fjallgard and use internal conflicts to his advantage.Halvard welcomed Sigvard with open arms,

promising him everything he had always wanted:plenty,power and a life of luxury.In Halvard's camp,situated on the edge of the Forest of Shadows,Sigvard had everything he lacked,choice wines,abundant food and beautiful women,paid for by the apparent generosity of King Halvard.Feasts were frequent,and every night was a feast for Sigvard, who seemed to have found here the right place to live his carefree life.But behind this continuous feasting,Halvard hatched his treacherous plans,wanting to conquer the kingdoms of Fjallgard and Iskali.The king Halvard gave Sigvard the privileges he wanted,but at the same time made sure to keep him in his own net of influence.He urged Sigvard to use his resentment towards his family and accept the idea of an alliance to weaken King Ragnar.In this way,Halvard could more easily take control of Fjallgard and eventually reach the throne of Iskali,with the king's renegade son on his side.Sigvard,blinded by ambition and resentment,he agreed, seeing in Halvard a father figure and a mentor who could help him recover his place in the world.King Halvard,learning about the imminent wedding between Princess

Freyja and Prince Eirik, decided to play his last book, setting up a treacherous plan to destabilize the alliance between the two kingdoms. To this end, he sent his daughter, Princess Ingrid, known for her captivating beauty and mysterious gaze that could charm anyone, but also for his manipulative and treacherous character. Ingrid had long black hair, intense green eyes and an enigmatic aura that immediately attracted attention, but beneath her angelic beauty was a dark soul, ready to hurt in order to gain power. Halvard was aware that Ingrid could become an irresistible temptation to Eirik and thus destroy his promise to Freyja and ruin the unity between Fjallgard and Iskali. One cloudy morning, Ingrid set off on her favorite horse, a black stallion named Skadi, towards the border of the kingdom of Fjallgard. Skadi was a stately horse, with a mane as glossy as obsidian and piercing black eyes, as mysterious as his master. The princess wore a cloak of black velvet, and in her gaze was an unwavering determination. Her plan was to gain Eirik's trust, deceive him and make room for his father in the kingdom of Fjallgard.

As she made her way through the forest,Ingrid made sure she appeared on the path that Prince Eirik and his cousins,Bjorn and Leif,often rode during their training.That morning,Eirik,Bjorn and Leif were on the path near Alvdal lake,chatting and enjoying a short break.Suddenly,the sound of galloping horses broke the silence forest,and they noticed a mysterious figure that seemed to be coming towards them in a hurry.Ingrid reached them with a troubled expression,feigning indescribable fear.She jumped off Skadi,and the horse calmed down near the lake.Eirik he looked at her in amazement,noting her striking beauty,but also the disturbance on her face,while Ingrid approached him with a trembling voice:

- Please,help me! I was attacked by thieves on the road,they tried to rob me! I managed to escape,but I don't know where I am... Please,I need help.Eirik turned his gaze to Bjorn and Leif,then,in a determined tone,asked her:
- What is your name,miss,and how did you get here,in such a remote forest?

- I'm Ingrid...from a noble family on the edge of your kingdom,she answered,with a trembling voice.I was riding as usual,but on the way I was attacked and...I got lost. If you don't help me,I will stay here at will fate...Eirik felt caught between his duty to help her and the restraint he felt.Ingrid's intense and enigmatic gaze disturbed him,and at that moment,without realizing it,he felt a strange attraction for this unknown who seemed to be in a desperate situation.

- You will be safe with us,Eirik told her,offering her his hand to help her climb back onto Skadi.As they walked towards the castle in Fjallgard,Bjorn and Leif looked on skeptically and worriedly,suspicious of the unexpected appearance of this mysterious princess.However,Eirik could not hide his fascination with her,a fascination that Ingrid noticed and which she planned to use to lure him into her trap.Arriving at Fjallgard Castle,Ingrid was immediately taken to the doctor to be examined,and within the massive walls of the castle,her story began to spread.The doctor,a man The old man,known for his wisdom and skill,began to examine her,but found no signs of injury to suggest a recent battle.However,Ingrid,already having a plan well in place,began to simulate a state of fatigue and weakness,and when the doctor withdrew to talk with King Ragnar,Ingrid used the moment of solitude to implement her strategy.

Seizing the opportunity,Ingrid approached Eirik,who had been watching her worriedly the whole way,and she let herself look vulnerable,her eyes wide and sad at him.Before he could react, she clung to his neck,seeming to find refuge in his arms,and began to whisper to him:

- My savior...I can't even imagine what would have happened if you hadn't found me... He paused,letting a tear roll down his cheek.

-My name is Ingrid and I come from a noble family from the edge of the kingdom,and my father is a merchant.

On the way, I was attacked by thieves and kidnappers, who tried to catch me and take me to unknown places...I don't even want to imagine what could have happened to me...Prince Eirik listened to her attentively, troubled by this story. Her presence and the enigmatic charm of the girl awakened in him a feeling of compassion and a strange fascination, and he he said to him in a gentle voice:
-Ingrid, you are safe now. We will do our best to find those who tried to harm you. Looking at her intense green eyes, Eirik felt himself more and more caught in her spell, without- and he could tell that this was her intention. Ingrid continued, bowing her head slightly and looking more and more affected:
- I have no one here but you, Eirik... Everyone in my family is far away, and I... I don't know if I will ever be able to return home. Maybe destiny brought me here...
Eirik flinched at these words and felt a wave of compassion, even a sense of responsibility towards Ingrid. He gently squeezed her hands and assured her that he would make sure she got the protection

From a distance,Bjorn and Leif watched their interaction suspiciously.They had seen Ingrid's sharp look at that moment when she thought she was not being watched, and they had a hunch that the story she what he had said was nothing more than a carefully crafted lie. But for the moment,the two remained silent,determined to give Eirik time to discover the truth on his own.However,Ingrid swore to herself that she would conquer Eirik and that he will carry out his father's treacherous plan,regardless of the obstacles encountered.In the days that followed,Ingrid managed to establish herself at the court of King Ragnar,where she created an aura of a vulnerable and mysterious noblewoman.The King and Queen Astrid was treated as an honored guest,and Eirik was more and more fascinated by her beauty and enigmatic charm.In a very short time,Ingrid became the presence he could not do without,always being around him and gaining his trust every day.But behind her sweet smile and green eyes that always seemed moist with emotion,Ingrid was constantly working on her plan.During her days in the castle,she was attentive to every detail related to the defense and the customs of the soldiers,and at night,when everyone was asleep,he went to a gate behind the royal palace,where he met a horseman and through him sent news to King Halvard,reporting every weakness discovered.One morning,Ingrid and Eirik they were walking in the garden of the castle,admiring the blooming roses.Eirik,feeling closer to her,asked her in a moment of sincerity:

-Ingrid, you are so mysterious...I feel that you keep many things hidden.Could you tell me more about your family,about the kingdom you come from? Ingrid sighed theatrically,bowing her head and looking overwhelmed with sadness.She quickly embraced the role of victim and began to tell Eirik an emotional story made up on the spot.

-My kingdom is small and powerless,Eirik…we are a noble family that no one has heard of and we are constantly in danger.My father is a powerful man,but he has no powerful allies,so all he does is to defend ourselves.That's why I came to ask for help from King Ragnar…In fact,I don't even know if I'll ever be able to return home… maybe this is my place.
-Ingrid looked down and Eirik feeling more and more disturbed by the young woman's apparent vulnerability,he took her hand and said with sincere gentleness:
-You are safe here,Ingrid,and you will always be welcome at our court.Bjorn and Leif,who witnessed this scene from the shadows,exchanged a suspicious glance.They were increasingly suspicious of Ingrid and they sensed that her intentions were not nearly as pure as she tried to make them seem.

Chapter -4 Betrayal comes from Vornheim Kingdom

One quiet night,Eirik's two cousins decided to put their suspicions to the test and started following Ingrid.Noticing her strange behavior and the frequent times she seemed to disappear from the castle rooms,they suspected that she had hidden connections.At one point,they saw her sneaking out of the castle and heading towards the south gate of the palace,where she met the mysterious rider as usual.Bjorn then had an idea:they waited for Ingrid to leave the gate and they saw how a horseman with a black hood on his head was galloping away,they quickly mounted the horses that were prepared for the daily routine,and went in pursuit of the mysterious horseman.Unfortunately,they could not reach,but they were close enough to see the insignia of the Kingdom of Vornheim and knew where the spy was coming from,the fact that the message was intended for King Halvard.

-Exactly as I suspected,whispered Bjorn,full of anger.

- This is nothing but a spy who has come to divide the kingdom.Leif clenched his fist,looking at his cousin with iron determination.

-We must tell Eirik,warn him.We cannot allow this schemer to break his connection with Freyja and destroy our alliance with the kingdom of Iskali.At dawn,Bjorn and Leif decided to tell everything to him Eirik.They found him in the training room and,wasting no time,told him about the mysterious rider,explaining the suspicions they had from the beginning and highlighting the danger that Ingrid represented.Eirik listened in silence,but at the end of their story,his face darkened.

-It's hard to believe, but...we have to see if these accusations are true.I can't leave anything to chance.We'll organize a meeting and see if Ingrid will admit who she really is.In the evening,Eirik called

- Ingrid into the audience room,telling her that she wanted to discuss her plans to return home and her family.Ingrid,unsuspecting,showed up in a long,emerald green dress,trying to she plays the role of grieving

noblewoman.But this time,Eirik was cold and distant,and when he asked her for details about her family and the kingdom she came from,Ingrid began to lose her temper,getting confused in her answers,moment,Eirik revealed the message intercepted by Bjorn and Leif.

-What does this mean,Ingrid? Did you think you could lie endlessly and betray us from inside your own castle? Ingrid froze,but quickly regained her posture,trying to cast a spell on the prince again.

-Eirik,my dear, it's not what it seems...Everything I did,I did to protect myself.You're the only one who mattered to me here...But Eirik, now completely disappointed,crossed his arms,showing him that her charms had no more power over him.

-You made a big mistake by coming here and trying to divide us.Out of respect for King Ragnar, you will be imprisoned and judged,and our alliance with Iskali will be stronger than you ever thought.Ingrid was captured and taken to a cell in the basement of the castle,and word of her identity as a spy soon reached the ears of King Ragnar

and Queen Astrid,who decided to put her on public trial for treason.Eirik,though still slightly disturbed,felt freed from the dark influence of his Ingrid and resumed preparations for her marriage to Freyja,now knowing better how precious true love and loyalty were.News of Princess Ingrid's capture soon reached the ears of Sigvard,Eirik's exiled brother,who now lived under the protection of King Halvard,Ingrid's father.When Sigvard learned that Ingrid had been captured and imprisoned in Fjallgard Castle,he felt obliged to free her.Although disinherited,Sigvard still felt a deep connection to his home kingdom and an attraction to Ingrid,knowing her dark charms.King Halvard,being preoccupied with plans to conquer Fjallgard,saw in rescuing his daughter an opportunity to sow discord among the rival royal families and decided to give Sigvard the necessary support.Halvard sent five of his most good soldiers in his army,loyal fighters,trained in hand-to-hand combat and night infiltration.This team consisted of:Gunnar,an unrivaled archer;Torvald,a fearsome warrior;Vidar,the most agile and swift of them all;

Eriksen, a skilled strategist; and Stian, renowned for his endurance in any kind of battle. Dressed in dark clothing and carrying light weapons so as not to attract attention, Sigvard and the five soldiers set out under the cover of night, avoiding the main roads and passing through the dense forests on the border between the two kingdoms. Their journey was intense and hurried, each aware of the enormous risk they were taking in entering so close to the heart of the kingdom of Fjallgard. Sigvard was determined to get Ingrid out of captivity, and deep in his heart he wished he could win King Halvard's recognition for his act of bravery, hoping that one day he could take back what was once taken from him, perhaps even with the king's help. When they arrived near the castle, Sigvard and the soldiers hid at the edge of the forest, observing it from a distance. Being aware that, during the night, the guards changed their shifts every hour, they decided to take advantage of the moment of the changing of the guards, when vigilance was lower.
-Sigvard, we need to know exactly where Ingrid is kept, said Gunnar, the archer, pulling on his hood and preparing his bow.

-If we find her quickly,we will be able to leave without leaving a trace.
- I know the place,replied Sigvard,who remembered the configuration of the castle from his childhood.
-Most likely,she is kept in the underground dungeon,under the north wing.Torvald,the strongest of them,proposed that they split up to distract the guards,while Sigvard,Eriksen and Vidar would sneak into dungeon to free Ingrid.The plan was risky,but it could definitely work,especially if no one suspected their presence.In the stillness of the night,the team moved nimbly through the shadows, avoiding the guards patrolling the castle's perimeter.When they reached the entrance in the dungeons,Vidar slipped a lever into the mechanism of the door, opening it silently.Entering quickly and silently,they descended the narrow stairs to the dungeon.Ingrid was waiting for them,as she suspected that her father or Sigvard had sent someone to save.When he saw them,a sly smile spread across his face.
-Sigvard,she whispered,stretching out her hands,I knew you would come.You are the only one who understands how unfair everything was!

-Let's get out of here quickly,Ingrid.We don't have time to waste,he answered,giving the signal to retreat.While they were retreating,a guard,who caught the movement of the group,started shouting for help.At that moment,the whole castle yard came to life,and Sigvard and his men had to fight to escape.Gunnar managed to shoot some of the guards with precision,covering the others,while Torvald and Stian dealt from the soldiers who were approaching too quickly.Sigvard and Eriksen fought side by side,making sure that Ingrid was protected in their center.Although many of the guards were trained to defend the castle,Sigvard's team managed to create a corridor through to emerge from the inner courtyard, fighting their way to the forest.Managing to escape from the castle and hide in the forest,Sigvard and his men celebrated their victory in silence.Then,wasting no time,they set out for Halvard's kingdom, knowing that they would be awaited with reward and hospitality.Arriving in Halvard's kingdom,Sigvard was welcomed as a hero,and Ingrid thanked him with a triumphant smile,promising her support in front of her father,who now saw in Sigvard an ally of trust.King Halvard was grateful and offered Sigvard's warriors wine, gold,and the promise of a bright future.In addition,Halvard reaffirmed his intention to carry out his plan to conquer the kingdoms of Fjallgard and Iskali.But Sigvard he wasn't content with just the reward and praise he received.Now,more than ever,he dreamed of regaining what he believed was his due:the right to the throne of Fjallgard and, perhaps,a future at the head of a united kingdom alongside Ingrid,who he felt more and more attached.While Halvard was gathering an army and strengthening his allies for the planned invasion,Sigvard and Ingrid,now with united forces,were building their own hidden dream,to gain supreme power over the northern kingdoms and take revenge everything they felt was stolen from them.

Chapter -5 The union of the two friendly kingdoms through the
marriage of Prince Eirik and Princess Freyja

King Ragnar,worried and disturbed by the news of Princess Ingrid's
rescue from his dungeons,organized a secret meeting with King
Harald,the father of Princess Freyja,at an old castle on the border of the
two kingdoms.In the council room,decorated with torches that lit
discreetly the stone walls,the two kings took their seats along the large
oak table,surrounded only by a few trusted advisors.Ragnar opened the
discussion directly,without detours,showing how deeply affected he was
by the recent events.
-Harald,things are much worse than I anticipated.My soldiers have
discovered that the man who broke into my castle and freed Ingrid is
none other than...Sigvard,my banished son,Ragnar said in a voice
hoarse with sadness and anger.
-Not only has he allied himself with King Halvard,but he has betrayed
his own blood,his own brothers,and intends to attack us.It is clear that
our enemy is not only lurking on the edge of the kingdom,but has also
infiltrated his own people between us.King Harald listened
attentively,sharing his ally's deep concern.
-It means that King Halvard orchestrated the whole situation to weaken
and divide us.And with Sigvard on his side,he now has a gateway to
your kingdom,Ragnar.We cannot allow our alliance to be weakened.We
must act before let them have a chance to attack us.Ragnar
continued,his face scowling.
-That is precisely why we must strengthen the bond between our
kingdoms,through Eirik's wedding to Freyja.Postponing this marriage
would be an unnecessary risk,and our family bond will deter any attack
from Halvard.We cannot afford any more hesitation.

The war is near,and we cannot fight as strangers.We will become one family and one front.Harald nodded,looking respectfully at Ragnar's decision.

-I agree.As soon as we get back to our courts,we will hold the ceremony.Freyja and Eirik must become one soul,to be not only princess and prince,but also the symbol of our alliance.We will show the whole world that we are united and that even King Halvard,with all his intrigues, cannot defeat us.The two kings then discussed the details of the war preparations.King Ragnar mobilized his best generals to organize the defense of Fjallgard Castle and decided to fortify the fortresses of near the border.He ordered more frequent patrols in the forests and on the roads towards Halvard's kingdom,determined not to allow another infiltration attempt to succeed.Meanwhile,King Harald began gathering additional troops from his kingdom,preparing to send soldiers to support Fjallgard Castle,in case Halvard achieves his goal and attacks from all sides.Messengers were sent to the most influential families and noble houses,asking for their help and loyalty for the

impending battle.In the following days,the courts both kingdoms entered the fever of preparations for the wedding,but also for the war.The news of the marriage between Princess Freyja and Prince Eirik brought hope to the people of both kingdoms,being seen as a promise of peace and stability in the face of the threat that was taking shape on the horizon.However,behind the festivities,soldiers were training incessantly, and fortifications were being checked and strengthened.Eirik and Freyja, although initially reserved about this political alliance,began to spend more time together and develop a sincere and trusting bond.Freyja,with her strong and wise spirit,was able to inspire Eirik to prepare himself to become a strong and determined leader.In turn,Eirik offered Freyja support and affection,and their love began to blossom,strengthening and even more the connection between the two kingdoms.In the days before the ceremony,Ragnar and Harald had a last meeting,this time with Eirik and Freyja.They explained to them how important their union was for the future of the two kingdoms and how decisive will be their alliance against King Halvard.

- My children, said Ragnar gravely, this marriage is not only about two hearts, but about a safe and free future for all our people. You must trust each other and fight together, because only by joining our forces can we confront the threat that looms ahead. Eirik and Freyja shook hands, promising each other loyalty and love, determined to defend their kingdoms together. Meanwhile, at King Halvard's court, Sigvard and Ingrid were preparing their own plans. Cornered by the imminence of war, they decided to make one last attempt to divide the kingdoms of Fjallgard and Iskali, before their alliance was strengthened by the marriage of Eirik and Freyja. Sigvard gathered some of his trusted men and, together with Ingrid, they began to work on a cunning plan, destined to cause chaos at the wedding ceremony and thus ruin the unity between the two kingdoms. With the wedding only a few days away, the tension was palpable. King Ragnar and Harald were preparing for war, and their alliance was about to be strengthened. However, somewhere, hidden in the shadows, Sigvard and Ingrid were plotting the latest, determined to destroy this moment of peace and bring war to the very heart of the kingdoms of Fjallgard and Iskali.

The story was approaching a confrontation decisive,and the alliance between Eirik and Freyja was about to be tested in the face of the greatest danger they had ever known.Dense around the kingdoms of Fjallgard and Iskali.King Halvard set up his sabotage plan,determined to stop any form of alliance between the two kingdoms.Together with Sigvard and Ingrid,he thought of a strategic attack that would strike right in during the ceremony,at a moment of maximum vulnerability.Sigvard, fueled by resentment and a desire for revenge, took it upon himself to sneak into the kingdom of Fjallgard,where he could join the crowd of guests coming to witness the wedding.Ingrid,for her part,agreed to accompany him,knowing that her charm and beauty would help her obtain any essential information from the courtiers or slip rumors that would turn one against the other.On the evening before the ceremony,the atmosphere in Fjallgard Castle was one of anticipation and excitement.The walls were decorated with gilded cloth and fine fabrics,and the inner courtyards resounded with the music of harps and flutes.Freyja,in her room,was dressed in a white dress,embroidered with silver threads, which the ladies of honor carefully arranged.

.Although she seemed calm,Freyja felt an uneasiness that did not give her peace,like an echo of an unseen danger.At that moment,one of her cousins,Astrid,entered the room.Noticing the restlessness in Freyja's eyes,he asked her:

-Freyja,what happened? Aren't you happy? Freyja answered him in a calm but pressing voice:

-It's more than happiness,Astrid.It's a strange feeling,like the calm before the storm has settled over the castle.It's like something dark is waiting at our gates.Astrid tried to calm her down,reminding- and that although King Halvard and Sigvard are dangerous,their kingdoms are now united.However,his words did not dispel the fears of Freyja,who felt that the night would bring more than a ceremony.That night,Sigvard and Ingrid met in a clearing at the edge of the forest near Fjallgard castle.Accompanied by King Halvard's most loyal soldiers, they planned the last attack and prepared to infiltrate the castle.

- My sister is a perfect prey for Eirik,said Sigvard,with a bitter smile.
-But we'll see how durable this alliance is after we're done with them.On their wedding day,they will be busy and vulnerable.Ingrid,looking at the pale lights of Fjallgard Castle,half smiled.

-The whole kingdom will be preoccupied with the wedding,and we will hit exactly where it hurts the most.We will destabilize them,we will set them friends against friends and then we will run away,leaving them to destroy each other.Their plan was simple,but devastating:in the midst of the ceremony,Ingrid and Sigvard would mingle among the guests and slip treacherous lies about the intentions of the kingdom of Fjallgard,spreading gossip about a possible betrayal of King Ragnar.Then,at the climactic moment,a group of Halvard's soldiers would launch an attack on the inner court,causing panic and chaos.The next morning,the sky was covered in deep gray clouds,bringing with it a cold and gloomy atmosphere.However,the ceremony was going

to take place,and the guests had gathered in the great hall of the castle.Despite the uneasiness that was felt in air,King Ragnar and King Harald were determined to see their children united and thus seal their alliance.During the ceremony,Ingrid and Sigvard slipped through the guests,smiling and complimenting everyone,but subtly spreading rumors of a possible betrayal on the part of King Ragnar.
-Did you hear that King Ragnar was secretly discussing with another power? Maybe this marriage is just a strategic move to control Iskali,Ingrid whispered,under the guise of a joke.
At one point,a group of soldiers loyal to Halvard,disguised as nobles,approached the great hall,ready to strike at Sigvard's signal.When the ceremony reached its climax,Sigvard threw a discreet signal towards them.The soldiers launched a sudden attack,throwing swords and arrows into the crowd of guests.Panic immediately broke out,and the guests began to flee in all directions.Eirik and Freyja were pulled from the crowd by the guards and taken to a safe room.King Ragnar and King Harald immediately ordered the soldiers to repel

the attack,and many of the infiltrating attackers were captured.Sigvard and Ingrid,however,quickly slipped into the chaos created,fleeing into the night.With King Ragnar and Harald's soldiers victorious in the face of the attack,many of Halvard's conspirators were captured and interrogated.Eventually,many of them revealed details of Halvard's plans and connection to Sigvard,and the truth came out.Ragnar and Harald reunited in a crisis meeting and,this time,without hesitation,they decided to join forces and start the war against King Halvard.Before leaving,Eirik and Freyja swore to each other that they will stay together regardless of the dangers,united by the desire to face the danger with their people.The war that was going to take place would change the destinies of the two kingdoms forever,and the alliance between Eirik and Freyja was not only a union of love,but and one of blood and fire.

Chapter -6 Revenge of the Prodigal Son Sigvard

The days following the attack on the wedding were marked by tension and intense preparations for war in both kingdoms.The news of Sigvard's betrayal and his alliance with King Halvard spread quickly,and the royal courts of Fjallgard and Iskali became veritable centers of military command.Eirik and Freyja,who had now officially begun their lives as husband and wife,swore to defend the two kingdoms together,and their bravery and loyalty quickly made them seen as symbols of hope in the face of an uncertain future.Late one evening,while they were conferring with the military commanders,a messenger brought a sealed letter for King Ragnar.The seal was unmistakable:it belonged to Sigvard.Curious and alert for any trap,Ragnar opened the letter and began to read.It was a surprisingly calm letter,in which Sigvard asked to meet his father in an isolated place on the border of Halvard's kingdom.He challenged Ragnar to come unarmed and talk "as father and son."King Ragnar he looked at Eirik and Freyja,who were by his side,wondering if it was wise to answer Sigvard's call.
- It could be a trap,said Freyja,with a note of concern in her voice
-But if there is even a chance that Sigvard has reconsidered his betrayal,this may be an opportunity to prevent bloodshed.After a long discussion,Ragnar decided to accept the meeting,but he took precautions.The edge of the forest,where he was to meet Sigvard,he would be accompanied by several of the best archers,who would remain hidden among the trees,ready to intervene if anything looked suspicious.On the morning of the meeting,the mist covered the ground like a thick cloak,and the silence of the forest was deep.Ragnar reached the meeting place first and waited.

After a few moments, a figure appeared from the mist: Sigvard, dressed in a dark cloak, with a dark and proud look. Although his figure was shadowed by the tall hat, Ragnar immediately recognized his son's eyes, they were cold and calculating but still had a glint that reminded him of the child he once raised.

- Father, said Sigvard, with a fake smile.

-Thank you for agreeing to meet me. I felt the need to explain why I chose this path. Ragnar looked at him with a pain mixed with anger and disgust.

- What do you have to say, Sigvard? You chose to side with our greatest enemy, King Halvard. You chose to betray your own blood for power. Sigvard laughed softly but bitterly.

-Oh, father, you always saw me only as a shadow, as a failure. All I did was forge my own path. Halvard welcomed me when you banished me. In his kingdom I found a new family, a new power. And now, when I saw how you entrust everything to Eirik, did you need me?

-You are blinded by resentment, said Ragnar, trying to remain calm.

-You chose to join a man who only wants destruction and conquest.Halvard does not see you as a son.He is using you to destroy the house we built together.Sigvard smiled mockingly.
-Perhaps,but now I have something that Halvard doesn't have:an unconquerable lust for revenge.And I didn't come here to make peace,father.I only came to tell you that the end of your kingdom is near.At that moment,Sigvard drew a small sword,but before he could make a move an arrow from among Ragnar's archers flew,striking Sigvard in the hand and causing him to drop the sword.Rana stopped him and with a glare and full of bitterness,he retreated into the shadows of the forest,disappearing before Ragnar's men could catch him. After that disturbing encounter,Ragnar returned to the castle determined to do everything in his power to protect his kingdom.Heartbroken by his son's betrayal,together with Harald he organized a meeting of all the nobles and commanders of both kingdoms,preparing for the inevitable battle. Eirik and Freyja,seeing the troubled state of King Ragnar,assumed the role of maintaining morale soldiers and courtiers.

They organized festivities,where courage and hope were celebrated,and their words inspired the soldiers to defend their land.When King Halvard's troops reached the borders of the kingdom of Fjallgard, they were met by a united army,at the head of which stood Eirik and Freyja,wearing the shining armor of the lords of the north.The battle that followed was fierce,and the sound of swords and shields echoed over the dark hills and forests.In the midst of the battle,Eirik came face to face with Sigvard,and their duel was one of life and death.Sigvard,with a hatred accumulated for years,struck with uncontrolled violence,but Eirik,confident and calculated,managed to defend himself and keep his composure At one point,Eirik disarmed Sigvard and, with his sword at his throat,said:

-Your betrayal has brought us pain,but you do not have the power to destroy us.I invite you to return and repair what you have ruined.This is the last chance I offer you.Sigvard,overwhelmed with anger and shame,and- he bowed his head and murmured:

-Never.And so,Eirik had to face him to the end,ending the fight with a decisive blow.With the death of Sigvard and the retreat of Halvard,the kingdoms of Fjallgard and Iskali remained united.The victory over the common enemy strengthened the alliance between Eirik and Freyja and brought peace and stability.Following the war,the two young men were officially crowned as heirs to the united kingdoms,promising to rule in the spirit of justice and wisdom.The memory of the struggle and sacrifices made to protect the two kingdoms of became a legendary story,which would be passed down from generation to generation.

Chapter-7 Kingdom of Fjallgard-Iskali

After the victory against King Halvard and the end of Sigvard's treachery,the kingdoms of Fjallgard and Iskali enjoyed a rare peace,but the atmosphere still carried the echoes of war.Meanwhile,Eirik and Freyja,with surprising wisdom for their age,began to repair the weakened bonds and rebuild the fortresses destroyed in the battles,uniting their kingdoms around a common vision of peace and prosperity.However,amid the restored tranquility,a deep mystery would once again attract the attention of the young rulers.One night cold winter,Freyja had an intense dream,an almost overwhelming vision:a black wolf with fiery eyes appeared at the edge of a forest,followed by a snowstorm and harsh winds.In the dream,the wolf raised its head to the sky and a long howl,as if it were the warning of a new threat.Then, a voice of unnatural clarity whispered to him:
- The danger has not yet been completely banished.The shadow envelops the fallen one,and the enemies in the shadow sharpen their teeth.Upon awakening,Freyja,shaken by this vision,shared it with Eirik.The dream seemed more than a simple manifestation of anxiety,

it was like an omen from ancient times,and Eirik recognized the significance of the black wolf: the symbol of an evil lurking,ready to strike from the shadows.Deciding to investigate,Eirik and Freyja turned to the wisest learned and most skilled sorcerers in both kingdoms,hoping to find answers.At the castle in Fjallgard arrived an old sage known as the Eldar Master,who carried within him the ancient secrets of the Nordic kingdoms.The Eldar told them of an ancient prophecy that spoke of the "Blaming Wolf",a troubled spirit that haunted the sons to the guilty,trying to cause a collapse of the royal line.

-In death,some spirits of rebels do not find peace,said the Eldar,and Sigvard's spirit may now be part of this restlessness.Without a ceremony of forgiveness and relief,he could remain trapped between worlds.Eirik and Freyja decided to organize a journey to the place where Sigvard had fallen,in the heart of the dark forest,to perform the ritual of unburdening recommended by the Eldar.But the forest was deeply imbued with Halvard's energy and the dark memories

of betrayal,and the shadows of the past seemed to follow him at every step.One night,while they were setting up camp,a strange noise came from the heart of the forest.Freyja and Eirik got up in alarm and saw,beyond the flames of the campfire,a familiar figure:it was like a vague shadow of to Sigvard.The spectral figure seemed to be troubled,and her eyes seemed to burn with a smoldering rage.
-Sigvard,Eirik whispered,filled with regret and pain,why can't you find peace? Sigvard's ghost,with a burning look and a spectral voice,said:
-Peace will come only when the one who pushed me to betrayal is defeated.Halvard promised me power,but left me a prey to pride and humiliation.Until his spirit disappears from these lands,I too will not find peace.These words were enough for them to understand what had to be done.King Halvard,who had fled after the defeat and was hiding in hidden corners of his kingdom, was still a threat that needed to be removed.Eirik and Freyja decided to join forces once again,alongside the bravest warriors of Fjallgard and Iskali,embarking on a final expedition to end Halvard's tyranny and influence.

Along the way, Sigvard's spirit guides them, showing them the hidden routes and secret lairs of the army of Halvard. Finally, they reached a fortress hidden in a dark valley, where Halvard had gathered the last remnants of his army. The final battle was intense, but the leadership and courage of Eirik and Freyja triumphed. At the last moment, Halvard was confronted by Eirik, who, with a single blow, ended his tyranny. With Halvard's death, the dark shadow surrounding the kingdoms of Fjallgard and Iskali dissipated, and Sigvard's spirit could finally find peace. Back in their united kingdoms, Eirik and Freyja celebrated this victory with their people, knowing that peace had finally settled on the land. They assumed the role of rulers of a new united kingdom, and promised that no the shadow of the past will no longer be able to darken their path. Under their rule, the kingdom prospered, and the spirit of peace and unity spread among the people. The stories of their battles, betrayals and victories turned into legends that would inspire generations to come. With wisdom and strength, Eirik and Freyja

kept their promise to protect their people and ensure that the shadows of the past never return. After the fall of Halvard and the establishment of peace in the united kingdoms, Eirik and Freyja dedicated themselves to rebuilding and the strengthening of the alliance between Fjallgard and Iskali. A new era of peace seemed to be settling in, but the lives of kings never remain peaceful for long. As they worked to strengthen alliances with neighboring kingdoms and restore infrastructure, rumors began to appear about a new danger coming from the far frozen north, a mysterious and little-known land. Unknown messengers began to arrive at the court of kings Eirik and Freyja, bringing stories of a mysterious force that reigned in the frozen north, over fjords and hard-to-reach mountains. An old legend spoke of a forgotten tribe known as the "Children of the Eternal Snows" who lived in the heart of the coldest mountains and worshiped ancestral spirits. What caught Eirik and Freyja's attention were rumors of an unknown leader, a powerful and enigmatic being called Stigandr, "The Wanderer", who had united the

isolated tribes and seemed to plan an expansion into the southern kingdoms.In the royal court,intense discussions began.Freyja and Eirik were aware that a war with the northern tribes might destroy their newly reunited kingdoms.However,they were determined to find out the truth, and that meant a dangerous journey north to meet and,if possible,negotiate with Stigandr.Eirik and Freyja decided not to send a mere soil north.They decided to travel themselves to show respect to the mysterious tribes and achieve a peaceful settlement.Together with some of their most loyal men and with the help of the old Eldar Master,who knew the Norse rituals and traditions,they set out on the expedition them, leaving the kingdom in the care of advisors and close relatives.The road through the north was wild and dangerous,and the cold,blizzard and wild animals put them to the test many times.Accompanied by the Eldar,who brought with him a vast experience in understanding Nordic culture and spirituality,they passed through isolated villages,where they were offered shelter and warned of Stigandr's mystical power.

In some villages,the elders spoke of him as a living god,a man chosen by the spirits of the north to unite the tribes,but also about a mysterious priestess who advised him and who had the gift of reading the future from the shadows of fire.When they arrived at the foot of the mountains in the north,Eirik and Freyja were greeted by a delegation of warriors clad in furs and armed with spears of ice and iron.They led them through dark passages and frozen forests to Stigandr's main camp, an imposing settlement in the heart of the mountains, protected by a barrier of ice massive.On a throne carved in stone,Stigandr was waiting for them.He was a tall man with snow-white hair and ice eyes,who seemed to be half human,half spirit.Stigandr looked long and hard at Eirik and Freyja,and a harsh and ancient wisdom seemed to shine in his eyes.After a long silence,he spoke to them:

-You have come from afar,to our cold and wild lands.Why should I negotiate with those who have defiled these lands with your presence?

Eirik kept his composure and answered him respectfully:

-We are here not to conquer,but to keep the peace.Our kingdoms have suffered from war and betrayal,and we want a bloodless future.We want to understand your purpose and find a way to live in harmony

Stigandr crossed his arms and glanced at his priestess, Alvhild, who was whispering something in his ear.Then he said:

-Peace is only possible if you recognize our sovereignty over this northern land.The Children of the Eternal Snows have never submitted, and they will not now.To prove that their intentions were sincere,Alvhild,Stigandr's priestess,suggested that Eirik and Freyja to pass a test of courage and wisdom,an ancient ritual called the "Trial of Ice and Fire".It was a test that involved crossing a frozen lake at night,under the light of the northern lights,and going through an underground tunnel,where the fire it burned in stone-carved fireplaces

fueled by the essence of the earth. Any royal couple who passed this test earned the respect of the northern tribes but no one had succeeded in hundreds of years. Eirik and Freyja accepted the challenge, determined to prove their devotion to the united kingdoms. With every step on the frozen lake, they felt the weight of their past, and in the tunnels of fire, they had visions of their lovedones who had perished in the battles But together, hand in hand, they endured the cold and the heat, remembering the love and loyalty that gave them united. Finally, exhausted, they came to the surface and bowed before Stigandr and the priestess Alvhild, who, with a solemn look, recognized them as leaders worthy of the Nordics' respect. With this test passed, Stigandr agreed to sign a peace pact, and the Children of the Eternal Snows pledged to keep their territories in exchange for their freedom to observe their ancestral customs. The Nordic tribes became hopeful allies for the kingdoms of Fjallgard and Iskali, and, for the first once, a solid alliance was established between the northerners and the kingdoms of the south. As they returned home, Eirik and Freyja felt that all the fallen pieces had finally returned to their place.Peace was now more than a wish,had become a reality won through courage and sacrifice.The years that followed were years of prosperity for all the united regions.Under the rule of Eirik and Freyja,the story of the battle,the alliance and the peace achieved turned into a lesson for the following generations.Their courage and wisdom,trials and victories,have become not only legends,but landmarks of life for all the inhabitants of the united kingdoms.

Chapter-8 Legends of the North

The years passed and the unified kingdom prospered under the leadership of King Eirik and Queen Freyja.The peace and stable alliances seemed unshakable.But in the silence that reigned over the kingdom stories had begun to circulate of a different threat,one unseen but yet felt by all:an ancient prophecy,forgotten by many,but rediscovered by the old Eldar.It spoke of a time when the "shadow of the immortals" would try to return and bring chaos back to the northern lands.On a cold winter's night,when winds howled across the mountains,the Eldar Elder demanded an urgent audience with the king and queen.With a worried look on his face,he began to tell them about an ancient and dark magic once used by some spirits known as the Shadow Immortals.These immortals,gods forgotten by the times,had the power to control not only people,but also nature itself,causing natural disasters and unleashing wild creatures on those who threatened their existence.

- It is said,said the Eldar,that the Immortals have retreated into the depths of the world,but their power can be awakened through a forbidden ritual.Recently,I discovered ancient writings that suggest that followers of this magic began to gather in hidden places,

seeking powers that no one should wield.Freyja and Eirik,though determined to keep the peace,knew they had to investigate these rumors.With the support of the Eldar,they decided to consult the wisest figures in the kingdom,including the priestess Alvhild,their ally from the north,and other tribal elders from the Children of the Eternal Snows.A group of loyal warriors,along with the Eldar and some Nordic mages,set out with Eirik and Freyja in search of places where these mysterious followers might gather.They crossed the isolated lands and snowy forests,arriving at the edge of the frozen north,where a network of caves and underground tunnels hid traces of unusual activity.One night,while their camp was quiet,Freyja sensed a strange presence.An a chill ran down his spine,and a shadow appeared in front of him that seemed to be of human form.
-Why do you come to our places? whispered the voice,which seemed to come from all directions.
-Nothing good lies here for you and your kingdom.Eirik and the others jumped to her defense,but the shadow disappeared as quickly as it had appeared,leaving behind an unnatural coldness and a grave message:

-The earth will be awakened,the fire will burn again.As they advanced through the dark galleries,they discovered a series of ancient inscriptions,which spoke of the "Ritual of the Rebirth of the Immortals".The Eldar,wise and brave,realized that for to face this power a sacrifice was required to stop the ritual, and that sacrifice had to be made even by someone who knew the ancient magic and the meaning of the prophecies.In the depths of the cave,they came across a gathering of followers,chanting powerful incantations around a green flame shining. Eirik, Freyja and their men prepared to attack,but the Eldar stopped them for a moment.

-A sacrifice is required to untie the bonds of this ritual.If I do this,the shadow will disappear,but I will no longer be here to help you.Take the power of my knowledge and carry it forward.Without thinking,The Eldar spoke his last incantations with unwavering courage.The green flame died down under his words,and the followers,disoriented and weakened,were captured by Eirik and Freyja's men.

When the fire died down,the Eldar's body disappeared like a mist ,remaining only an ancient symbol of protection and knowledge,a sign of his sacrifice for the kingdom.With the sacrifice of the Eldar,the kingdoms were freed from the threat of the shadow immortals.Returning home,Eirik and Freyja instituted an annual festival in honor of the Eldar and protective spirits,honoring not only the memory of those who fell,but also the spirit of unity and knowledge passed down through the generations.The kingdoms of Fjallgard and Iskali remained united and,under the wisdom of Eirik and Freyja,became an example of prosperity and peace for all realms around.Their legacy would last through the ages,and their story,full of courage and sacrifice,would be told to children in every corner of the kingdom,as a symbol of the continuous struggle against the shadows that threaten peace and harmony.The years passed in the kingdom unified, and the festival dedicated to the Eldar had become a symbol of gratitude and unity.Under their wise rule,Eirik and Freyja strengthened alliances and ensured peace,and the kingdom prospered.However,the shadows of the past had not entirely disappeared,and the vestiges of power left by The effects of the Shadow Immortals would still be felt, as their offspring would face trials of a more subtle but equally dangerous nature.Eirik and Freyja now had two children:a daughter,Liv,and a son,Arvid.Liv was gifted with a keen sense of justice,and the knowledge and wisdom of his parents seemed to him a never-ending spring.Arvid,though younger,showed a special curiosity towards ancient legends and stories of lost magic.From a young age,he was drawn to the kingdom's forgotten rituals and symbols,always open to discoveries and questions.One day,while exploring the palace's old library,Arvid found a scroll carefully hidden behind some old tomes.

On the scroll,the words seemed to be written in an ancient alphabet, covered in strange symbols.The words,written in the archaic Norse language,seemed to describe "The Call of the Immortals" and "The Secret of the Eternal Snows".Fascinated,Arvid decided to keep the scroll hidden, for he felt it was the beginning of a greater story,one of the kingdom's roots and hidden powers. Liv and Arvid ventured on a journey to the northern tribes,seeking answers about the symbols on the scroll.The now elderly priestess Alvhild received them with respect and led them to a hidden sanctuary,an ancient place where the Children of the Eternal Snows kept their sacred secrets.There,Alvhild revealed that the scroll found by Arvid contained ancient incantations,a call to Immortals who,though weakened, could be awakened by power-hungry minds and hearts.

-Every kingdom,said Alvhild,has its share of shadows of its past.Those who once sought the power of the Immortals have not disappeared altogether,but have retreated to hidden places,where they continue to hunt the ignorant.Arvid,must know that not all knowledge brings wisdom,and not all mysteries are worth unraveling.Calling the shadow can prove dangerous,and the faint of heart risk becoming victims of their own curiosity.Arvid remained fascinated by the ancient secrets,but Alvhild's warnings had their left its mark on him. Together with Liv,he swore to use any knowledge he gained only for the good of the kingdom.In the years that followed,Liv and Arvid returned home,carrying with them not only the memories of their mysterious encounters,but also a determination renewed to defend the kingdom.They have dedicated themselves to peace and wisdom,aware that their future depends on the balance between courage and prudence.The story of the royal family continues,shrouded in mystery and illuminated by a legacy of sacrifice and love.And in the long, cold nights,the people of the kingdom look to them with trust,knowing that, like their parents,Liv and Arvid will be the guardians of a future where power is governed by wisdom, and peace is sought at the cost of any sacrifice.Time passed,and Liv and Arvid grew up,preparing -se for the responsibilities of the kingdom.Despite their efforts to bring peace and prosperity,the shadows of the past had not completely disappeared.Rumors of remaining followers of the Immortals hiding in isolated places and planning to bring back the old powers were spreading throughout the kingdom.Arvid he had become more and more interested in these mysteries,and Liv supported him,although she always made sure that her brother did not fall prey to the temptations of the unknown.One night,a mysterious messenger arrived at the castle in Fjallgard with troubling news.This was a man from a remote village in the north that had witnessed a series of unusual events:destroyed crops,unnatural winds that brought darkness,and strange sounds in the forests.The villagers had begun to believe that the spirits of the Immortals had awakened,and the seed of fear and insecurity was

was spreading rapidly. The messenger asked for their help, imploring Arvid and Liv to investigate these strange phenomena and bring peace to the kingdom. Eirik and Freyja, now respected and wiser rulers, decided that Arvid and Liv were ready to take over this mission. They organized an expedition, accompanied by a few loyal warriors and the kingdom's trusted advisors, to investigate the strange happenings in the north. Arriving in the remote village, they discovered an oppressive atmosphere and fearful villagers. After a few days of research, Arvid and Liv learned of the existence of a hidden group called the Shadow Schemers, led by an enigmatic leader known as Aksel. He was rumored to have once been a servant of King Halvard, but after his fall, Aksel swore revenge united kingdoms and master the ancient powers. Using ancient artifacts and relics, Aksel tried to reawaken an ancient magic that could control the will of people and change the course of nature. With the help of the locals and the knowledge gained from Alvhild and the Eldar, Arvid and Liv located the hideout of Aksel, in a cave hidden among the mountains. Entering the cave, they were greeted by darkness and an ominous aura.

Aksel, a tall man with long hair and a harsh gaze, awaited them in a ritual full of symbols and candles green, invoking the shadow of the Immortals.

- You came too late, laughed Aksel, his voice reverberating menacingly in the cave walls.

-The shadows have been awakened, and your kingdoms will pay for the betrayals and vain alliances you have made. I will take what was denied me and rule over the entire world! Arvid and Liv prepared for battle, but in time as they advanced, a faint light appeared between them, it was the symbol of protection left by the Eldar, now shining in memory of his sacrifice. Illuminating the entire cave, the symbol blocked Aksel's dark forces, and he seemed overcome with rage. With incredible boldness, Arvid and Liv used the knowledge they received from the Eldar and Alvhild to break Aksel's incantations, and the entire dark energy of the cave dispersed in an explosion of light and scattered shadows. Aksel's ritual was interrupted, and the Shadow Wizards were defeated. Liv and Arvid managed to capture Aksel and bring him before King Eirik and Queen Freyja to stand trial.Upon their return to the kingdom,Eirik and Freyja held a great gathering,where Liv and Arvid they were honored for their courage and devotion.They told everyone about the sacrifice of the Eldar,about the ancient dark forces and about the power of knowledge and wisdom.In their honor,it was decided that the symbol of protection left by the Eldar would be kept as the emblem of the kingdom unified,and the old teachings to be passed on to future generations to prepare them for any shadow that may appear.Thus,the kingdom of Fjallgard and Iskali remained united, protected by the courage of those who chose peace over power.And the legacy left by Eirik and Freyja,by Liv and Arvid,would live forever,forging a future where light and darkness coexist,but where wise men walk fearlessly,defending their lands and their loved ones.

Chapter-9 An Ancient Prophecy,The Eye of the Gods

After the victory over the Shadow Wizards and their return to the kingdom,Liv and Arvid received praise and recognition not only from their parents,but also from the entire people.Despite the triumph,a shadow of concern still lingered in the hearts of the two brothers.That Aksel had been defeated,something told them that the legacy of the Immortals was not completely extinguished.Eirik and Freyja,noticing their son and daughter's desire to protect the kingdom,decided to give them more knowledge of the ancient traditions and ancient alliances.They invited to the court sages and scholars from the farthest corners of the kingdom,people who knew the stories,rituals and ancient symbols,in the hope that Liv and Arvid would learn to recognize and prevent any potential danger.Liv,with her sharp mind and keen sense of justice,she learned about war strategies and political alliances,while Arvid, fascinated by mystical lore,studied runes and ancient Nordic

magic.Together,they formed a perfect team,able to approach any challenge with both reason and intuition.In a day,Alvhild,the old priestess,paid them an unexpected visit.Although age weighed her down, her eyes shone with deep wisdom.She brought them an ancient amulet,known as the Eye of the Gods,which she said could reveal the truth hidden from any liar.It was a sacred object,which only the wisest of priests and queens used in ancient times.Before leaving,Alvhild said to them:

-An old prophecy says that,in the moment of greatest balance,the Eye of the Gods will show the way to the light of truth.Keep it close,for you will need it soon.Time has passed,and rumors have begun to circulate in the kingdom about a mysterious man,a charismatic leader,who gathered disaffected people on the northern borders.Liv and Arvid learned that this was Sigvard,Eirik's older brother,whom the kingdom thought was lost forever after the betrayals of his youth.With a charm diabolical and a carefully crafted story,Sigvard promised the people a freer and richer kingdom where everyone could live as they pleased.

Sigvard began to form an army of rebels,people who had once been subjugated by kings who had served the Immortals.Luring them with crafted words and false promises,he dreamed of overturning Eirik's throne and taking over the unified kingdom.One dark night,Liv and Arvid were awakened by the sound of battle horns.Sigvard's army had arrived at the castle gates Fjallgard.Along with their parents and allies in Iskali, the brothers prepared for defense.In the midst of the battle, when the safety of the kingdom seemed lost,Arvid took out the Eye of the Gods and pointed it at a group of warriors from Sigvard's army.Shone with a blinding light, revealing the true face of the people gathered by Sigvard.Many of them were nothing more than slaves to the manipulation and dark magic of the Shadow Wizards.Seeing the truth, some of them gave up the fight and sought escape,disarming the the others.The amulet's light continued to shine,strengthening Eirik and Freyja's soldiers and revealing the wiles of Sigvard's strategy.Sensing that he was losing the battle,Sigvard tried to flee,but was caught by Arvid and Liv.In front of King Eirik and the entire kingdom,Sigvard was sentenced to exile,this time forever,and his evil influence was completely removed from the kingdom.After Sigvard's threat was removed,the kingdom was restored,and the people continued to live in peace.Under the leadership of Liv and Arvid,Fjallgard and Iskali flourished,building a society based on justice,knowledge and respect for ancient wisdom.The story of the two brothers,their parents and the sacrifices made to defend the kingdom remained in the memory of all.The Eye To the gods it was preserved as a symbol of justice,and Alvhild's prophecy was passed on as a warning for the future:Those who seek power without wisdom and those who manipulate light and darkness will pay,for truth will always triumph.

Thus, in the long winter nights,when people gathered around the fire,

the story of Eirik,Freyja,Liv and Arvid was told with pride and admiration,reminding everyone that the unified kingdom was built on sacrifice,courage and love.The years they passed quietly after the banishment of Sigvard and the triumph of Liv and Arvid,and the kingdom of Fjallgard-Iskali prospered under their rule and that of their parents,King Eirik and Queen Freyja.Under the protection of the Eye of the Gods,alliances strengthened, and peace and wisdom they kept the balance in the kingdom.One deep winter night,when the moon was covered with thick clouds and the cold seemed to freeze the air,Liv had a powerful dream,a vision that disturbed and attracted her at the same time.In the dream,a forest mysterious figure appeared in front of her,immersed in a thick fog,and a gentle but firm voice whispered to her:

-It is time to step into the unknown,daughter of the kingdom,for the past still has untold stories and ancient shadows must be faced to release the full light.Search for the roots of your kingdom and you will discover the hidden power of the ancestors.Liv woke from the dream,disturbed by its intensity.The entire next day,he shared his

vision with Arvid,who listened intently,convinced that it was a particularly important messageTogether,they decided to search for answers,sensing that there was something their ancestors had not discovered,and that the past it had secrets left undiscovered.Liv and Arvid sought advice from their parents,who told them that such a forest did indeed exist,on the distant border between Fjallgard and an ancient realm known as Midgard,which was the legendary place of their families' origins.Norse royalty.There,the old forests guarded the ruins of ancient temples where,it is said,long ago they worshiped forgotten gods and goddesses.The two brothers gathered a small escort of their best friends and a few devoted warriors and they headed for the dream place. On their journey they encountered majestic landscapes,from snow-capped mountains to crystal clear lakes,and the dense forest welcomed them with a sacred silence.Before long,they arrived at an ancient stone gate carved with runes ancient signs that seemed to watch over the hidden realm even today.Once they entered the heart of the forest,Liv and Arvid discovered the Temple of the Gods,

hidden for thousands of years,covered by thick ivy.In the center of the temple,they found an altar and a stone inscribed with forgotten words:Those who seek to protect and bring the light must become one with their ancestors, to understand not only the light but also the shadow that accompanies each step.At one point,a shadow rose from the altar and took the form of a wise figure,their ancestor Skadi,who had once been a great warrior and guardian of this sacred place.In a soft voice,he spoke to them of forgotten times, of the power that once dwelt in Fjallgard and Iskali,and of a legend of an undivided force that can unite all five northern realms if used wisely.

-In you, heirs of the united kingdom,lies the seed of true power,that of unifying and guarding the realm against all the darkness that may come.But this power demands a price,a sacrifice of a fragment of yourself,a total dedication to those you serve.After receiving this wisdom,Liv and Arvid returned home stronger and wiser.For several months,they worked together with their parents to create a coalition between all the northern kingdoms,an alliance that would not only keep the peace,but actively watch over the safety of every family and every commoner.Each kingdom was of agree to send delegates and trained soldiers to establish the Eternal Guard,an organization to defend the Nordic alliance,based on the teachings Liv and Arvid received in the Temple of the Gods.And so,their kingdom became a symbol of wisdom and unity, leaving a a legacy of courage and justice that would endure for generations to come.

Chapter-10 Liv and Arvid Future Monarchs

Years passed,and Liv and Arvid,driven by their responsibilities as future monarchs,strengthened Nordic alliances and traveled through the allied kingdoms to learn more about their people.With each journey, the bonds between the kingdoms grew stronger,and the Eternal Guard it was proving its usefulness to the full,fending off any external threats and ensuring peace.In a harsh winter,dark rumors began to spread.Several travelers coming from the south told of a mysterious figure,known as the Frozen Shadow,who conquering territories and gathering loyal soldiers with unusual speed.Anyone who refused to join was enveloped in a deadly cold, as if winter itself were this leader's ally.King Eirik and Queen Freyja called an urgent council, inviting all allies to attend.In the throne room of Fjallgard, the leaders of the Nordic kingdoms gathered to debate solutions and plan defenses.But fear hung in the air,as no one knew for sure who this new enemy was and what powers he possessed.During the council,Arvid proposed to investigate the Temple of the Gods itself to learn more about the Frozen Shadow.Liv agreed to accompany him,remembering that Skadi, their ancestor,had said that there were other mysteries hidden there that might not have been fully discovered.The two brothers once again ventured into the Forest of Beginnings.Although the forest seemed peaceful,a strange coldness hung in the air,as if nature itself sensed the danger.Upon entering the temple,Liv and Arvid found new symbols that had not been there on their last visit.Engraved in stone,the symbols seemed to come to life,and a pale light emanated from them.With the help of the Eye of the Gods,the brothers deciphered a message that spoke of the Frozen Shadow:an ancient warrior,cursed to wander the realms forever

frozen,seeking power and revenge.The temple also stated that this warrior had an unshakable hatred for the northern kingdoms and was now returning to fulfill his old desire to conquer the realms and plunge them into an endless winter.Back in the kingdom,Liv and Arvid told everything they had discovered to their parents and allies.With a well-planned plan,the Eternal Guard and allies prepared for a final battle against the Frozen Shadow,but they knew that more was needed more than weapons to defeat an enemy with supernatural powers.

Liv, guided by the Eye of the Gods, decided to seek an alliance with the spirits of the ancestors in order to receive their blessing and strength in battle.Arvid,on the other hand,intensively studied Nordic magic, discovering a particularly powerful protective spell,but which required a personal sacrifice.On a cold night,the brothers went to the altar in the Temple of the Gods and swore that they would defend the kingdom at all costs.The spirits of the ancestors accepted the sacrifice and blessed them,giving them special protection against the powers

Frozen Shadows.When Frozen Shadow and his army arrived in front of Fjallgard,a fierce battle began.The Shadow Army seemed unbeatable,but the Eternal Guard and allies fought bravely.Liv and Arvid used the blessing of the ancestors and the power of the Eye To the gods,and slowly,the enemy soldiers began to retreat.Finally,the brothers faced the leader himself,the Frozen Shadow.Beneath his fearsome appearance,they saw a man trapped in a curse, but powered by a hatred born of betrayal.Liv offered him one last chance to break the curse and retreat,but the Shadow refused.With their combined power and the sacrifice required,Liv and Arvid managed to break the spell that- it gave him power,freeing the Frozen Shadow from his curse.His army dispersed like mist in the wind, and the kingdom was finally at peace.After this victory,Liv and Arvid became legendary heroes,and the kingdom of Fjallgard-Iskali forever remained a symbol of unity and courage.

Chapter-11 King Eirik and Queen Freyja,had ended their journey in this world

On a solemn day,the kingdom of Fjallgard-Iskali was overcome with sadness,because the old monarchs,King Eirik and Queen Freyja,had ended their journey in this world.A grandiose procession was organized,and all the nobles of the northern kingdoms,the leaders of the alliance,loyal and noble families gathered to say goodbye to those who protected them with devotion and love.On that day of mourning,when Eirik and Freyja were to be laid on the funeral pyre,a phenomenon happened strange.From among the crowd,a murmur arose,and the people moved aside as a dark,mysterious figure appeared at the edge of the forest.That figure seemed familiar,but no one dared to speak its name.While the figure approached,an oppressive silence fell,and people began to whisper:

-Sigvard...The renegade son,returned from the shadow of the two realms! Sigvard looked ageless,as if the years spent away from life and death had not affected him at all,but his face was darker,his eyes colder,and a shadow of bitterness and sadness darkened his gaze.According to Norse legend,the princes of noble lineage who lose their lives through family betrayal are caught between the two realms,and if the time comes for the surviving brother to pass away,they can appear at the funeral,bound by a powerful fate magic.Liv and Arvid,as and the whole crowd,were shocked by the appearance of Sigvard.The people did not dare to approach,but his younger brothers faced his gaze without fear.In a serious and imposing voice,Arvid asked him:Sigvard,why did you come? You left this kingdom years ago,leaving us only the memory of your betrayal and the shadows of the suffering you brought upon our family.Sigvard answered in a deep,reverberating voice,as if speaking from the depths of a dream:

-No noble soul can remain in peace when justice has been defeated by the shedding of brotherly blood.I was bound to this place and to you, just as my ancestors were bound to the dust of this land. I came not to bring suffering,but to close a story and restore a balance between us.Queen Freyja,beyond unforgiving life and death,has always been known as a protector of truth and justice.Liv and Arvid,remembering their mother's teachings, and - they looked at Sigvard,looking for a deep sincerity in his eyes.In turn,Sigvard took out a small silver medal,a symbol of those who have fallen from honor,and knelt in front of his parents' funeral pyre.

- This medal is proof of my sins and mistakes,said Sigvard.
-I accept my fate and repent for the loss and pain I have caused.But I was called here to end the cycle.Accept these words and this humility to allow my spirit to find rest.Liv and Arvid,recognizing that revenge and old hatreds no longer had a place,they searched in their hearts for a way to end this dark chapter.Standing up beside Sigvard,Liv put her hand

on his shoulder and said:
- We,the children of our parents,are not only the heirs of a kingdom,but also of the lessons of love and justice that they left us.Forgiveness is our final gift,because only in this way will our kingdom remain united and without shadows.Arvid added:
- We forgive you,Sigvard, not for you,but for the peace of the kingdom and for all those who have suffered from the wrongs of the past.With these words,a deep peace fell over Sigvard. The crowd looked on with respect and amazement,feeling that they were witnessing at a unique moment of healing and ending a cycle of suffering.At that moment,Sigvard's body began to disappear,disappearing into a pale light,like the morning mist.His spirit was released and his soul finally stepped into a land of peace,leaving behind an eternal memory of the power of forgiveness.The funeral pyre of King Eirik and Queen Freyja was lit,and the fire rose to the heavens,guiding the two kings to the land of the ancestors.Thus ended an era,and Liv and Arvid became the true monarchs of the unified kingdom,preserving the legacy of their fathers and the wisdom of forgiveness.With their hearts cleared of burdens and new hope in their eyes,the two continued to lead their people towards a future of peace and prosperity.

Chapter-12 Kingdom of Vintergard and Kingdom of Stormheim

Arvid,the brave king of Fjallgard-Iskali,began his expedition through the five kingdoms of the North,eager to know the traditions,riches and people of each land.Besides exploring the kingdoms,Arvid knew that one of the heiresses of these kingdoms was to become his wife,thus strengthening the alliance between them.Each kingdom was distinct,with its own values and powers,and the king of each land hoped that his daughter would be Arvid's chosen.The kingdom of Vintergard,the northernmost of all,was dominated by snowy mountains and forests of pines that seemed endless.The kingdom was ruled by King Torvald,a leader renowned for his wisdom and loyalty to his allies.His daughter,Princess Astrid,was known for her adventurous spirit and hunting ability.Astrid had light hair,blue eyes and a fearless nature,being considered one of the bravest princesses of the North.The kingdom of Vintergard,located at the northern end of the known world, was an almost mythical land,where winters seemed endless and the cold wind made its presence felt even in the milder days of summer.Although the climate was harsh and the natural challenges constant,Vintergard was a kingdom of dramatic beauty,and its inhabitants prided themselves on their resilience.It was a vast land covered in endless pine forests,where snow fell early and it melted late,and the Semetian mountains rising to the sky formed a natural barrier,defended valiantly by their people.King Torvald,the ruler of Vintergard,was a respected figure not only in his own kingdom,but also in all the other kingdoms of the North.He was a man of imposing stature,with a snow-white beard and a penetrating gaze.His calm nature and wise words made him an admired leader,and his people gave him unconditional loyalty.Torvald was not only a ruler,but also a a skilled strategist,and his decisions

were always balanced and well thought out.His wisdom had earned him the reputation of the "Soul of Wintergard" because he was able to combine the needs of his kingdom with the interests of his allies.Torvald was also known for his keen sense of justice and loyalty towards the allies.Despite the harshness of the place, he was not an aggressive or conquering king, but a defender of the integrity of his kingdom.Torvald understood how important the alliance with the other northern kingdoms was and did everything in his power to maintain peace and stability in the North,even if it sometimes meant giving up certain resources or finding diplomatic solutions in tense situations.Wintergard was truly a wild kingdom,surrounded by tall mountains,covered in snow most of the year.Askr and Skogur mountains,called by the people "Ice Giants",represented the emblem of the kingdom,and the stories about the mysterious creatures hiding in their valleys were passed down from generation to generation.These places,often haunted by Nordic legends and myths, were considered sacred,and the people he had a special respect for them.Among the mountains were small villages

inhabited by brave hunters and miners,people who knew how to live in harmony with the harsh nature.The forests of Vintergard were vast and full of wild life:silver wolves,white bears and great stags roamed those places, and hunting was a means of survival and tradition.However,the people of the kingdom never hunted more than they needed,maintaining a careful balance between man and nature.Wintergard was known for its tall pines and hardwoods,resistant to the cold,which craftsmen used to create some of the most sought-after weapons and tools.King Torvald's daughter,Princess Astrid,was known throughout the Nordic kingdoms for her adventurous spirit and indomitable courage.Astrid was a young of an authentic Nordic beauty,with light hair and intense blue eyes,which seemed to reflect the coldness and intensity of the Nordic sky.Her nature was unique;a combination of fearlessness,curiosity,and sensitivity to nature.Astrid was no ordinary princess, but one who knew how to defend her kingdom and live by the traditional values of Vintergard.Raised among hunters and warriors,Astrid learned from childhood wielding the bow and stalking prey through dense forests.

There was no forest or mountain in Vintergard that she did not explore,and her people loved her not only for her beauty but also for the fierceness with which she defended them.She was known as a great huntress,and although she also mastered other crafts,hunting remained her greatest passion.Astrid had a special bond with the creatures of Wintergard,and even though she was an accomplished huntress,she knew when to protect and preserve the balance of nature.She had a saying:

-Before the mountain and the beasts,we are all equal,and this respect for the environment she lived in made her loved and respected not only by humans,but also by hunters and healers.Life in Vintergard was deeply connected of ancestral traditions and respect for nature and divinity.Every winter solstice,the people of Vintergard celebrate the Fire Festival,a celebration meant to encourage the sun to return and bring spring.On this night,residents light torches and torches and dance around fires to celebrate the light in the midst of darkness.Another important tradition was the Ritual of the Roots,a custom kept by priests in temples hidden in dense forests.They worshiped the roots and trunks of ancient trees and prayed for the prosperity of the forest and the animals that lived in it.Every family in Vintergard had a protective tree,an old pine under which they gathered in moments of balance to ask the advice of the ancestors.Even though it was located at the northernmost point and had a strong autonomy,Vintergard enjoyed friendly and strategic relations with the other northern kingdoms. King Torvald, being a wise leader,maintained diplomatic contacts and was often consulted by his allies,due to his reputation as a balanced ruler.The northern kingdoms found in Vintergard a reliable partner,even if he did not engage directly in military alliances.The union of the northern kingdoms was, however,a hope for King Torvald,who saw in strong alliances the best solution for maintaining peace.His connections with Skoglund and the other northern kingdoms were supported by his wisdom, and the people of Vintergard supported the idea of peace and collaboration,even in hard times.The kingdom of Vintergard remained not only a land of snow and endless forests,but also a symbol of Nordic courage,traditions and wisdom.Their people lived with devotion to their ancestral values and kept the belief that,no matter however great the hardships,union with nature and respect for mountains,trees and beasts was the key to survival. Princess Astrid,through her brave spirit and loyalty to her people,had become a representative figure of Vintergard.Young,but strong and wise,she he vowed to carry on the legacy of his fathers and remain a role model for his people,continuing to fight for the balance between man and nature in the frozen heart of Vintergard.Further south lay the kingdom of Stormheim,famous for its dramatic landscapes and gusts of winds that blew incessantly over the plains and lakes.King Harald,ruler of Stormheim,was an authoritarian man of frightening severity,but respected for his balance and justice.

.His daughter,Princess Signe,was a charming young woman,noted for her grace and beauty.Signe had a calm but extremely determined nature and a deep understanding of Nordic politics and rules.

The Kingdom of Stormheim,nestled between expanses of stony plains and deep lakes,was renowned for its dramatic landscapes and unrelenting winds that seemed to be rooted in the very bowels of the mountains.This kingdom had a wild beauty and a charm that seemed carved by the rough hand of nordic nature.The landscapes here were always imposing,with heavy and massive clouds crossing the sky in a ceaseless dance,accompanied by the winds that never stopped beating on the expanses of stone and cold waters.King Harald,the absolute master of Stormheim,was known throughout the northern kingdoms as a ruthless leader and respected for his ability to maintain order and balance.Harald was a tall and imposing man,with a harsh face scarred from his youth,and his voice had a force that shook even the most tough warriors.In Stormheim,discipline was strict,

and Harald made sure that anyone who broke the rules of the kingdom or disobeyed the will of his king was punished severely.But although his reputation as a harsh and severe ruler was well known,the people respected him deeply.Harald had a deep understanding of justice and balance, and his decisions,though sometimes harsh, were always right.He was the kind of king who did not compromise and who,above all,believed in the virtue of responsibility.Despite his strictness,Harald was a fair and incorruptible monarch,and was respected by both his subjects and neighboring kingdoms for this keen sense of justice.Stormheim enjoyed a wild and untamed nature,a kingdom defined by vast expanses of stone-covered plains and low bushes,where the winds blew incessantly and the vegetation adapted to the harsh climate.Cold and dark lakes,some deep and mysterious,were dotted among these plains,and their waters reflected the massive and sometimes ominous clouds in the sky.On the rare calm nights in Stormheim, the bright waters revealed the star-studded sky,but most of the time,gusts of wind and small waves created a gloomy and dramatic

picture.In Stormheim,the people were rough and tough, accustomed to the harsh and unpredictable life of this kingdom Norse.Their culture was deeply connected to the lakes and plains,and the wind,considered a sacred element, was respected and revered as a manifestation of the spirit of the kingdom.The winds of Stormheim were said to be the voice of the ancestors,whispering to them stories and memories of the past,and that they carried the wishes of the people to the gods of the North. King Harald's daughter,Princess Signe,was a young woman of captivating beauty and a presence that captured the hearts of all.Signe had light blond hair that seemed to shine as brightly as the ripples of lakes in the moonlight,and eyes a deep blue like the cold water of Stormheim.She was known for her natural grace and understated beauty that set her apart from the other Nordic princesses.But Signe was not just a charming young woman;she was a strong woman,endowed with remarkable intelligence and a deep understanding of politics and the rules of the kingdom.Raised under her father's guidance,Signe developed a determined character,

having a calm but extremely determined nature.She knew the situation of her kingdom well and could analyze every political situation with a lucidity rarely seen in young people her age.Signe had a deep loyalty to her father and to the people of Stormheim.Although it is said that a woman must be gentle,Signe did not hesitate to express her opinions and defend her positions in front of the court,even if they seemed unusual.Her determination and subtle understanding of politics made her a figure respected by the king's advisers and the people from Stormheim,who saw in her a leader with potential.In Stormheim,the wild nature and harsh climate played a central role in the lives of the inhabitants. Strong winds were considered sacred,and the people of Stormheim held special ceremonies called the "Festival of Winds" to celebrate this natural phenomenon.During this festival,residents would light torches and offer symbolic sacrifices to the gods,hoping that the winds would protect their kingdom and will bring prosperity.Another important aspect of Stormheim culture was their connection to the cold,deep lakes,considered to be portals to the world of spirits and ancestors.Once a year,during the long winter nights,the people of Stormheim the famous "Night of the Lakes",a celebration dedicated to the memory of the ancestors and the protection of the kingdom.On this night,each family would go to the nearest lake and throw a flower or personal object into the water,as an offering and symbol of gratitude for the departed. Stormheim,although a powerful kingdom,was isolated due to his position and harsh natural conditions.Despite this,King Harald knew how important it was to maintain alliances and diplomatic relations with the other kingdoms in the North.Harald was respected and often sought out for his advice by the other kings,because his wisdom and ability to make difficult decisions made him an invaluable adviser in the face of the challenges of the time.Signe,being an intelligent and politically well-trained princess,understood the importance of these alliances and was often involved in diplomatic meetings alongside her father.Her ability her ability to observe political subtleties and discuss things calmly and rationally made her a staple in diplomatic councils,and this skill was valued by neighboring kingdoms.Signe strongly believed that peace and cooperation between the northern kingdoms was essential to maintaining stability and prosperity,and she was willing to offer her hand in diplomatic marriage if it was necessary for the good of her kingdom.The kingdom of Stormheim,with its grand landscapes and the steadfast spirit of its people,was a harsh but beautiful jewel of the North.Harald,through his just and stern rule,brought balance and security to the kingdom, and Signe,through her grace and intelligence,promised to carry on her father's legacy.The people of Stormheim were deeply attached to the traditions and values of the kingdom,and Princess Signe,though a gentle and charming young woman,she was determined to keep this legacy alive.

As Signe continued to support her kingdom and fight for peace and stability in the North,the future of Stormheim looked promising,and the balance won by King Harald was maintained with highly valued by his people.

Chapter-13 Kingdom of Iskeborg and Kingdom of Skoglund

The kingdom of Iskeborg,located between deep fjords and clear waters, was ruled by King Bjorn,a great diplomat and strategist.Iskeborg was famous for its seafarers and for its impressive fleet,which protected the Nordic trade. The heir to the kingdom,Princess Ingrid,was a young woman with black and green-eyed, respected for her intelligence and skill in maritime tactics.Ingrid was known for her impetuous personality and ambition to expand the kingdom's fleet,dreaming of new trade routes and expeditions.Deep and clear waters, where mountains rose steeply along the coasts,and the cold waves of the northern sea carefully carved the contours of the land.Seen as a strategic and economic stronghold,Iskéborg was not only a prosperous and well-defended kingdom,but also a a place of exploration and trade,where maritime culture was ennobled and passed down from generation to generation.Its people lived for centuries in symbiosis with the sea,and King Bjorn,a skilled diplomat and great strategist,wisely watched over this unique Nordic kingdom.Bjorn,the ruler of Iskeborg,was known for his sharp mind and diplomatic spirit that brought him countless alliances and friendships between the kingdoms of the North.A king with extensive war experience and a good strategist,Bjorn was valued for his ability to anticipate the movements of his opponents,but especially for the ability to build lasting alliances,which strengthened the stability and prosperity of his kingdom.Under Bjorn's reign,Iskéborg became a center of trade and an important pole of influence

in the region.More than that,Bjorn he knew the people well and not only respected their traditions,but also encouraged their development.He strengthened diplomatic relations with neighboring kingdoms,frequently organizing assemblies where he managed to negotiate treaties and ensure peace,even in troubled times.Although temperamental and sometimes with unyielding accents,Bjorn was considered a just and caring king,and his vision of turning Iskéborg into a major naval force guided him over the years.What set him apart from other kings was his ability to use more than just the sword,but also words as weapons.Iskéborg was famous throughout the Nordic region for its strategic position between steep fjords and for its natural harbors that served as shelter for warships and merchant ships. Navigating these waters was considered an art, and the people of Iskéborg they were masters of the seas and shipbuilders second to none.In the harbors of Iskeborg,hardwood was skillfully fashioned into stately ships, and the sailors were known for their ability to maneuver the ships even in the stormiest northern waters.The War Fleet of Iskeborg,known as the

"Guardians of the Fjords",was not only one of the most numerous in the North,but also among the most feared.Always ready to protect their kingdom and maintain control over the trade routes, these brave sailors were the heart and soul of the kingdom,men who considered the sea their home.Trade was essential to the prosperity of Iskéborg,and Bjorn understood that protecting the sea routes and expanding influence the trades of his kingdom were essential to the well-being of his people.King Bjorn's daughter,Princess Ingrid,was a young woman of captivating beauty and a strong personality,known throughout the region for her skill in naval strategy and maritime tactics.With her jet-black hair and green eyes that seemed to reflect the depth of the fjord waters,Ingrid was an unforgettable sight.But more than her physical beauty,what attracted people was her impetuous and ambitious spirit,a combination of her father's courage and love of the sea,on who had inherited it from his family.From a young age,Ingrid had been fascinated by ships and maritime strategy.

She often joined the kingdom's fleet on sea expeditions,learning from veteran captains and sailors the art of navigation and naval warfare.Intelligent and calculating,Ingrid was not limited to simple travel experience,but she also studied strategies from historical naval battles and wanted to bring innovations to Iskéborg's fleet.One of her great ambitions was to expand the kingdom's fleet and open new trade routes, dreaming of expeditions beyond the known borders of the North.To her subjects,Ingrid was admired for her wisdom and determination,being considered a leader in the making,a woman who could not only take over the reins of the kingdom,but also lead it to new heights of glory.Sea,and sailors were honored and respected in society,being considered the pillars of the kingdom.Among the traditions of the kingdom was the "Festival of the Sea",an annual festival in which the entire population celebrated their connection to the sea.During this festivity,warships and merchant ships left at sea,decorated with colorful flags,and sailors and residents lit candles and made offerings to the gods of the sea for protection and abundance.

Another important tradition was the "Sailor's Oath",a ritual by which young men who aspired to become sailors took a solemn oath of loyalty towards the kingdom and protecting its waters.This oath symbolized their commitment to defend their country and serve the sea with dignity and courage.The ritual took place on the rocky coast,under the gaze of the captains and veterans,and after taking the oath,the young people received their first leather bracelet,which they wore with pride.Under Bjorn's leadership and with the support of his daughter Ingrid,Iskéborg was in a period of commercial expansion.The king aimed to expand the influence of the kingdom of along the coasts of the North and open up new trade routes that would allow a closer connection between the northern kingdoms and the other realms.Bjorn's ambition and diplomatic skill had already opened many doors,and Ingrid took it upon herself to make his dream a reality.She knew that a strong fleet would not only ensure the protection of the kingdom,but also strengthen Iskéborg as a trading hub,vital.In her quest to bring prosperity to the kingdom,Ingrid established a patrol system that ensured the safety of trade routes and limited piracy, making Iskeborg a safe place for all traders.However,her ambition went further,Ingrid dreamed to expeditions beyond the known realms,to the exploration and discovery of new territories that could bring even more riches and opportunities to Iskeborg.As Ingrid perfected her maritime and tactical knowledge,and King Bjorn strengthened his diplomatic relations,the future of the kingdom looked brighter.Shining as ever.The impressive fleet,the skill of the sailors and the ambition for maritime expansion were transforming Iskéborg into a great Kingdom.

In the heart of the North,surrounded by thick forests and lakes full of fish,was the kingdom of Skoglund,ruled by King Vidar.Vidar was a gentle and peace-loving monarch,and Skoglund was a prosperous kingdom,valued for its wealth of natural resources and skill in crafts.His daughter,Princess Liv,was a young woman of understated beauty and an empathetic nature,talented in the art of healing and knowledge of plants.Liv was loved by the people for her kindness and gentleness,and Arvid was impressed by her warmth and wisdom them.The kingdom of Skoglund was a real oasis of tranquility and natural beauty,located in an area with dense forests,clear lakes and wooded hills.Under the reign of King Vidar,Skoglund had become not only a center of economic prosperity,but also a bastion of traditions and Nordic values.King Vidar was known for his gentle and wise nature,and his people considered him a true father of the land,being one of the most beloved monarchs in the history of the kingdom.The true wealth of Skoglund came from the generosity of his land, but also from the good and hardworking souls of the inhabitants.Vidar was a gentle king with a deep-rooted wisdom and an open heart to his people.Coming from a family of leaders respected for their justice and calmness,Vidar was raised in the spirit of patience and compassion.

The monarch was a consummate diplomat and a good connoisseur of the needs of the common people,often being seen talking with the artisans,hunters or farmers of Skoglund to find out what their challenges were and how he could support them.Rather than imposing decisions,Vidar preferred to collaborate and to listen to the advice of the councilors and elders of the kingdom.Vidar was known not only for his balanced nature,but also for his wisdom in managing the natural resources of the kingdom.He was a supporter of forests,understanding that they were not only a source of wood, but also a habitat for wild animals,birds and rare plants,respected by the craftsmen and healers of Skoglund.He built sacred sanctuaries deep in the forests,places of silence for his people and symbols of the protection offered by the divinity over the kingdom.Skoglund was a kingdom of rare natural wealth.The forests provided hardwood,used in building ships and homes,and the kingdom's craftsmen had become famous for their woodwork,making fine furniture,sculptures and ornate weapons,which were in high demand.In all the other Nordic kingdoms.Birch and oak wood was used carefully,and the craftsmen of Skoglund

were recognized for their ingenuity and passion.The rich soil of Skoglund offered diverse crops:wheat,rye,berries and medicinal plants.The lakes of the region were stocked with valuable fish,and deer and wild boar hunting provided the necessary food for the people.Skoglund was also known for its springs of crystal clear water,which were said to have healing properties.In the middle of the kingdom,the central market was bustling,where merchants displayed local products and pilgrims from other lands came to trade and to seek the advice of the healers of Skoglund.King Vidar's daughter,Princess Liv,was the embodiment of Skoglund values and traditions.With a discreet beauty and a gentle soul,Liv was loved by her people and respected by all the noble houses in the North.She had brown hair,green eyes that seemed to reflect the forests around her,and a graceful yet charming allure in its naturalness and simplicity.Princess Liv she was renowned for her talent in the art of healing and her vast knowledge of the medicinal plants of the Skoglund woods.She spent many hours in the woods to Skoglund,gathering herbs and learning from the old healers.

Liv believed strongly in the power of nature and developed a deep respect for the plants and animals that populated the kingdom. Liv studied with well-known healers and shamans, and her wisdom and kindness brought- close to the heart of every inhabitant of the kingdom. When she learned of Arvid's visit, Liv was not interested in opulence or of his titles, but of his values and thoughts. Their meeting was a simple one, in the woods near the capital of Skoglund, where Liv told him about the art of healing and the soothing power of nature. Arvid was deeply impressed by her intelligence and empathy, seeing in Liv a similar spirit, but also a partner to support him in his ideal of bringing peace between the kingdoms. Skoglund also had a mystical side, keeping sacred traditions and places of worship in the middle of nature. Forests were considered sacred and were cared for by druids and priests who officiated ceremonies in sanctuaries hidden among the trees secular. Here, the people came to express their respect for nature and pray for rich harvests and health. The kingdom was crossed by rivers that flowed clear and fast, being fed by mountain springs.

These waters,considered sacred,were used in the purification rituals,and once a year,King Vidar himself,together with the priests, organizes a water purification ceremony,as a sign of gratitude for the gifts of nature.The culture of Skoglund was a harmonious blend of art,music and traditional dances.The crafts of the kingdom were highly valued in other northern kingdoms,and the woodwork and sculptures they produced were of rare beauty.Music was an essential part of everyday life,and traditional festivals were marked by the sound of horns and drums.Liv often supported artistic initiatives,encouraging the creation of a cultural center where the artists of the kingdom could express their creativity and transmit the traditions of the people.In this way,culture and the values of Skoglund were strengthened,offering a living example of harmony between man and nature.In relations with the other kingdoms,Vidar was always a balanced and respected negotiator.The neighboring kingdoms saw in Skoglund a reliable ally,and the union between Arvid and Liv reinforced this image of peace and harmony.Skoglund became the symbol of prosperity and peace,and trade relations with Fjallgard-Iskali intensified,contributing to the economic growth of both kingdoms.Through the wisdom of King Vidar and the gentleness of Princess Liv,Skoglund became a model of balance and respect for nature.Every inhabitant lived in peace and prosperity,and its forests and crystal clear waters continued to provide their people with their fruits.The legacy of Vidar and his daughter,Liv,marked entire generations,and the stories of their kingdom lived on,inspiring the kings and queens who they followed in the North.Skoglund remained known not only as a kingdom rich in resources,but also as a source of wisdom and kindness.

The kingdom of Solvik,located further south,was famous for its fertile plains and for the sun shining longer than in the rest of the northern kingdoms.King Olav,an optimistic and cheerful ruler,was known for his hospitality and generosity.His daughter,Princess Alva,was a young woman full of life and creativity,known for her love of art and Nordic traditions.Alva was a princess with an artistic nature,having a special talent in music and poetry.The kingdom of Solvik,located further south from the vast and cool lands nordic,it was an oasis of light and warmth.Spread across fertile plains and blessed with a mild climate,the kingdom enjoyed a prolonged warm season, a rare advantage among northern kingdoms.Solvik was a place of plenty,where grain grew healthy,and the fruits ripened under the benevolent rays of the sun.Here,the land was fruitful and well cultivated,and the people enjoyed a quiet,prosperous life and connected with the nature that surrounded them.King Olav,the master of this land full of light,was known throughout region not only for his leadership abilities,but especially for his optimistic nature and his generous spirit.Olav was a king who liked to be among his people,to listen to their stories and share their joys and worries.In the long evenings in the summer,he used to organize festivities in the fields, where people from all over the kingdom gathered to party together and dance under the starlight.The warmth of the king's soul and his gift for storytelling attracted everyone,turning each event into a celebration full of laughter and good cheer.Olav was also known for his hospitality.The doors of the palace in Solvik were always open to guests,and those who came to visit were treated to the choicest food and drinks.The palace,located on a hill overlooking fruitful fields,it was a beautiful and imposing building,decorated with paintings and sculptures that reflected the history and traditions of the kingdom.

Olav was proud of this place and its people and wanted to preserve the spirit of community and openness that characterized his kingdom. As king, Olav was a balanced and just leader. He had earned respect for his wise decisions and the way he resolved conflicts with empathy and understanding. This is how Solvik was seen as a peaceful and harmonious kingdom, and the people felt lucky that they had a ruler so close to their needs. Solvik was renowned throughout the North for its fertile plains and the natural beauty of its surroundings. The sun shone here more than in other kingdoms, and the rich soil and mild climate were perfect for growing grain, a of vegetables and fruits. The tall grain swayed in the breeze, and the orchards were full of fruit trees that yielded a rich harvest every year. In Solvik, agriculture was the basis of the economy, and the people were industrious and skilled at working the land. The kingdom was also known for its traditions and vibrant culture. Solvik had a strong inclination towards the arts, and music, dance and poetry were part of the daily life of its inhabitants. Every year, there were festivals dedicated to each season, and people gathered to celebrate the changes of nature, singing and dancing

until dawn.The dramatic landscapes and the friendly sun also inspired many artists,who painted scenes from everyday life,representing the beauty of the plains and the people who worked them.The daughter of King Olav,Princess Alva,was a lively and creative young woman,known and loved for her love of art and Nordic traditions.Alva was charming,with blonde hair like an ear of wheat and bright eyes,reflecting her passion for beauty and artistic sensibility.Raised in the middle of nature and inspired by the warmth of the kingdom,Alva had a special talent in music and poetry,and her voice was known by all who had the opportunity to hear her sing.Princess Alva was a being with an empathetic and joyful personality.She liked to be with his people and he often spent time in the villages,listening to people's stories and singing with them.He had a special talent for composing poems about the landscapes of the kingdom, about people's toil and about living in harmony with nature.Every morning,he woke up early to catch the sunrise,taking time to meditate and get inspiration for his creations.Alva wanted to keep the kingdom's traditions alive,which is why he frequently organized evenings of music and dance in the palace in Solvik.

These cultural meetings did not they were not only an occasion for entertainment,but also a way to bring people together,to celebrate their common identity.The princess had a circle of friends and artists who accompanied her on these occasions,and every meeting was marked by a story atmosphere,full of music,lyrics and joy.In Solvik,life flowed at a calm and benevolent pace,and the people of the kingdom went about their daily tasks with a positive and optimistic attitude.The kingdom was blessed with natural riches,but also with a close bond between the people and the rulers.King Olav and Princess Alva were seen as examples of generosity and harmony,traits that deeply influenced the culture and customs of the kingdom.Both the inhabitants and the nobles of the kingdom were proud with their hospitality and were known for their openness to all visitors.In particular,the traditions and festivals of Solvik had a special charm.The Summer Festival,one of the most anticipated holidays,brought together thousands of people who came from all over the kingdom to to participate in colorful parades,music and poetry competitions,and night parties under the stars.During this period,Alva became the soul of these festivities,dancing and singing with the people,instilling in everyone a sense of belonging and joy.With a generous leader and a talented and empathetic heiress, the kingdom of Solvik seemed destined to prosper and remain an oasis of peace and harmony in the North.King Olav's dream was for Solvik to become a center of art and culture in the North,a place where all neighboring kingdoms would come to learn,collaborate and celebrate together.He dreamed of a future where Solvik could become a symbol of beauty and peace,and Alva,his heiress,had the same vision.Alva wanted to create a sanctuary for artists,where people from all creative fields could come to be inspired by nature and contribute to the culture of the kingdom.

Thus,the princess planned to bring to Solvik masters of music,poets and painters who would contribute to the cultural and spiritual development of the kingdom.In this way,Alva not only preserved the traditions of the kingdom,but also brought a new and innovative breath,connecting the kingdom to the surrounding world.The Kingdom of Solvik,with its fruitful plains and its warm heart,kept alive the flame of harmony,and under the wise leadership of King Olav and the creativity of princess Alva,his future was bright,a model of peace and joy in the North.On his journey,Arvid spent time with each of the princesses,observing their qualities and values.He realized that each princess had a unique beautysp,ecial qualities and a heart devoted to his people,but a special closeness seemed to grow between him and one of them.

Chapter-14 Marriage of King Arvid to Princess Liv of Skoglund

After much thought,Arvid decided to choose Princess Liv of Skoglund.In addition to her empathy and warmth,he felt that Liv shared his vision for peace and harmony between the kingdoms.Their relationship was based on mutual understanding and respect, and the people of Fjallgard-Iskali looked forward to the wedding,knowing that this choice would further strengthen the Nordic alliances.Thus,by his choice,Arvid once again brought unity between the Nordic kingdoms,and the destiny of the North promised to be one of prosperity and peace under his and Princess Liv's reign.After Arvid officially announced his choice to marry Princess Liv of Skoglund,the Nordic kingdoms went into a state of celebration and intense preparations for the big wedding.All over the North,people began to decorate their homes with flags,fabrics and ancient symbols.

Offerings were made at the temples of the gods, and master blacksmiths, tailors and artisans worked tirelessly to create the most beautiful wedding gifts. At the royal court in Fjallgard-Iskali, Arvid and Liv spent their days in meetings with advisers, priests and nobles, preparing every detail for the ceremony that was to be the symbolic unification of the two kingdoms. Queen Astrid and Liv worked together on the wedding dress, and it was to be woven with gold threads and decorated with the ancestral symbols of The royal jewelers also made a special crown for Liv, made of silver and sapphires, symbolizing her purity and courage. King Arvid, in turn, organized a sacred ceremony in the temple of the ancestors to honor his parents, King Eirik and Queen Freyja. Praying for their blessing and for the peace of the kingdoms, Arvid promised himself that he would do everything to protect the people, honoring the agreements with the other kingdoms and strengthening the Nordic alliance. On the day of the wedding, Fjallgard-Iskali was invaded by the royal retinues from the other four Nordic kingdoms. Princesses Astrid, Signe, Ingrid and Alva arrived in great pomp, each bringing symbolic gifts from their kingdom:

bearskins and rare furs, handmade jewelry,rare wines and precious weapons forged by the most skilled smiths.On the day of the great event, the kingdom was decorated with torches and garlands of ice flowers,and the sound of horns and chants filled the air.The main temple was prepared for the ceremony,and the people of Fjallgard-Iskali and the other kingdoms gathered to witness the event that will unite their destinies forever.In front of the altar,Arvid and Liv took their vows before the gods,pledging faith and protection not only to each other,but also to the people and the Nordic alliance.Queen Astrid and the King Vidar,Liv's father,blessed them,and the priests concluded the ceremony with the ancient tradition of pouring a cup of wine on the ground,symbolizing sacrifice and the union of the blood of the kingdoms.When Arvid and Liv joined hands and stepped together out of temple,the crowd burst into applause and cheers of joy.For seven days and seven nights,the kingdoms celebrated their union.Every evening,banquets were organized with tables laden with game,fish and bread,and people danced around fires to the rhythm of songs performed by minstrels.

Shortly after the wedding, As Arvid and Liv began their reigns, they learned that in the southern North, a group of petty kings were forming an alliance against the united Nordic kingdoms. They were led by an ambitious leader named Harald the Storm, who hoped to destabilize the alliance. King Harald, who had not been invited to the wedding celebration, had expressed his dissatisfaction with the agreement between the Northern kingdoms and saw the marriage as a threat to his power. Arvid decided to send messengers to negotiate peace, but he was also prepared for any eventuality. Together with Liv, held a council with representatives of the five kingdoms to ensure that all resources are ready, and the alliance is strong enough to face potential dangers. Under the reign of Arvid and Princess Liv, the northern kingdoms experienced a period of peace and prosperity. The royal couple organized expeditions and developed new trade routes, and Queen Liv's teachings on plants and medicine improved the health of the people. Stories of their wedding became legendary, and the people revered them for their courage and wisdom, symbols of a new era of unity and power for the whole North.

Epilogue:
After the battles and betrayals that shaped the North and the union that brought peace, the kingdoms settled into a new harmony,one hard-won and sustained by alliances and promises.King Arvid and Queen Liv,chosen after a long and careful search,ruled wisely,wanting to leave behind a legacy of peace and stability.Together,they built an era in which each kingdom contributed to the common prosperity,and old rivalries were transformed into collaborations.The stories of King Halvard and Sigvard's treachery lived on in the immortal songs,reminding each kingdom that the thirst for power can lead to destruction.People spoke of the great battle that defeated the untamed ambitions of Vornheim,as well as about the wisdom of the five united kingdoms.Through deeds and words,Arvid instilled a new respect for the alliance between the kingdoms,and the old myths about the chaos and wars of the North became mere cautionary tales for future generations.Thus,the North remained united under one crown,but diverse and rich in their own traditions.The kings and queens of the future would bear this symbol of unity and lasting peace,seeking to rule their peoples with the same wisdom.Ultimately,history turned into legend,and the North settled,for the first time, in a lasting and glorious silence.

Copyright

(C)

Bucur Loredan 13-11-2024
Birmingham U.K.

Milton Keynes UK
Ingram Content Group UK Ltd.
UKHW031445261124
451586UK00011B/155